# Catch Me
# If You Can

J

# Look for these titles by
## *LB Gregg*

*Now Available:*

Trust Me If You Dare

# Catch Me
# If You Can

*LB Gregg*

SAMHAIN
PUBLISHING

Samhain Publishing, Ltd.
577 Mulberry Street, Suite 1520
Macon, GA 31201
www.samhainpublishing.com

Catch Me If You Can
Copyright © 2011 by LB Gregg
Print ISBN: 978-1-60928-102-1
Digital ISBN: 978-1-60504-950-2

Editing by Sasha Knight
Cover by Mandy M. Roth

First Samhain Publishing, Ltd. electronic publication: March 2010
First Samhain Publishing, Ltd. print publication: February 2011

# Dedication

To my husband, G.

# Chapter One:
# Keeping It Brief

*Jean Luc Pappineau*

*An Exhibition of Sculpted Works*

*Friday, 28 April*

*5:00-8:00 p.m.*

*Peter Stuhlmann Gallery*

*NY, NY*

I felt pretty damn good about the opening, until Shep McNamara strolled through the gallery door with a fresh new haircut and a spray-on tan and I aspirated the green olive floating in my martini. Fumbling my glass, I watched in disbelief as Shep sauntered by with a drink in either hand. I doubted he was carrying one for a friend. Sure, the drinks were free, but he didn't need to double fist. I coughed, trying to dislodge the olive, my chest seized, and Shep disappeared. What was he doing here? I coughed again, a little harder this time.

"You need help, Caesar?"

I shook my head at Brandon, our shirtless bartender, and hacked desperately into my soggy cocktail napkin. My nose watered; tears blurred my vision. The fucking olive wouldn't budge. I tried to expel it as gracefully as I could but it was...*lodged*...or something.

"Put your arms over your head," Mallory Albright instructed. The woman I most needed to impress this evening examined me through clever Lafont frames, her crimson lips pursed in concern. "That will lift your diaphragm."

She demonstrated by pulling her shoulders back and lifting her own diaphragm, one slender hand to her ribs. Her jet hair swung forward, making an angled point under her chin.

Normally, I'd have delivered a smart comment. Instead, I gasped, wheezed and banged on my sternum with a closed fist to no avail. That garnish wouldn't budge.

Brandon jumped the table to whack me on the back—the flat of his hand shoved me into Mallory. I horked up the olive, spitting it directly into her drink. She didn't flinch at the delicate *plop* it made on reentry or when droplets of gin spattered her bare arm. She merely flagged a waiter, who rushed over with a stack of paper napkins. He handed us both another much-appreciated martini, his silver tray dipping precariously close to the ornamental bust of Mayor Bloomberg.

Mallory set her dirty glass on the waiter's tray without acknowledging the remains of my olive. She peered over her glasses at me. "You're fine. Catastrophe averted. All better now, yes?"

"Yes. I beg your pardon." I dabbed my mouth with the cocktail napkin and then scrubbed the lapel of my new blazer. I glanced furtively around the perimeter of the room, searching the crowd for Shep and his deceitful cousin Poppy. That twit had promised me—*promised me*—she'd never invite him to one of my events.

I set my cuffs straight with a jerk and took a swig of liquor to settle my nerves and soothe my throat. No sign of either Shep or Poppy from my vantage point, but the urge to hide from one and kill the other had me shifting my feet restlessly.

Mallory continued to stare. "You're breathing fine now?"

Nodding politely, I rasped, "Yes, thank you, Mal," and carefully cleared my throat. "That olive must have gone down the wrong way." Much like me on the path to my career. Stuck at twenty-eight and barely making minimum wage. I'd have done better in the men's department of Saks or working in the restaurant with my pop and my brother. The art world didn't exactly pay well when you were in lower management.

Mallory looked thoughtful. "I knew someone who choked on a peach pit once—a girl at Smith. She scraped her esophagus and developed a bacterial infection. It turned into meningitis. She nearly died. These things happen sometimes. You didn't abrade anything, did you, dear?"

Abrade? "No. I'm just a little embarrassed, that's all. I'm sure the gin will kill any bacteria. Olives are soft. Don't worry about me, Mal."

"Oh, don't be silly. Sometimes we swallow wrong. You need to swallow slowly, dear." Mallory sipped her martini. She smiled with good humor at the bust of Howard Stern.

I couldn't possibly comment, although Brandon snickered.

"He could always practice swallowing," Brandon muttered.

I gave him an *I'm-paying-you* look, and he winked back at me but held his tongue. Brandon's massive pectorals gleamed with some kind of oil, but under the gallery lights he was beginning to show signs of age. He'd covered his gray, though he couldn't hide the crow's feet. Of course, they merely heightened his masculinity. "Shouldn't you be back at the bar?"

Mallory didn't spare Brandon a word. "It's a good turnout, Caesar. You've done a magnificent job putting together Jean's...*pieces*..." She said this as if she should finish her thought with the words "*of shit*" but was too cultured to do so. "I'm sure something will sell. The gin is flowing freely enough."

"It's flooding rather than flowing. Hopefully that will loosen people up to purchase." I needed for them to sell. Not for my boss or for Jean, but for myself. For my future. I wasn't proud of this, but I'd ride Jean and Peter's coattails to a better job if I could.

And tonight was the night. The gallery was clogged with well-lubricated art enthusiasts. Everything had been planned accordingly: the music festive yet discreet, the food excellent, the booze plentiful and the waiters mostly naked. Poppy and I had hoped that every girl and boy present would be amused. I was scheming to impress my targeted future boss, Ms. Mallory Albright of The Albright Gallery of Fine Art. She had no idea, but her assistant was about to give notice on Monday. I knew this because Steph had pulled me aside two weeks ago, at her own catered event, and said I could land a lucrative job if I didn't fuck up. My plan appeared to be working—until the olive.

I looked around for Shep. If I had a do-over, I'd aim that olive at his head.

Mallory took a delicate sip from her fresh glass, leaving a blood-red mark on its rim. Her fingers pinched the stem precisely. "This event must have cost a fortune. Did you adhere to your budget?"

"Somewhat," I hedged. "I called in a few favors."

That much was true. My family and friends may never speak to me again.

"I'm impressed. I don't think Peter understands how good you really are."

"He's been kind to me," I fibbed.

"Well, you let me know if he's unkind to you, and I'll set him straight." She patted my hand and floated away in her black eveningwear.

I took another look around the room. Brandon had returned to his station behind the bar, mixing cocktails with great flair. "Brandon, if you see Poppy, you inform her that I need to speak with her. Tell her to drop what she's doing and find me."

"Any message?" He speared an olive on a toothpick and flipped it into the air. It landed neatly in a martini glass.

"That was the message."

"Ah. Right."

I headed to the kitchen. I was five steps from the hall when a hand clapped me on the back, propelling me forward again. I caught myself on a patron, juggled my drink and pasted a smile on my face. "Oh, excuse me!" Somewhere in the room a camera shutter clicked.

Jean Luc Pappineau, the man of the hour, swayed drunkenly on his feet beside me. He'd lost his shirt, but his bow tie remained. His nipple rings gleamed in the gallery light. He might be in great shape at forty, but Jesus, what the hell was he doing? His smile was unguarded and his eyes were unfocused. Maybe we should cut back the flow of gin.

"Romano, what a night," he crowed.

"Yes. Congratulations. I'm pretty sure I've seen no fewer than six critics here." God help him. "Your name is getting recognition."

"Oh that's all shit, buddy. What we need is to make some sales."

"Excuse me?" I croaked. He was completely plowed. He had to be.

"You know—the dough. I need cash." He made the universal sign of money grubbing—that roll of his thumb along

13

the flat of his blunt fingertips. Jeez, there was nothing like a little avarice to make a true artist shine. He gave me a curious look. "What's wrong with your voice? You sound froggy."

"Must be the night air."

"Sounds like you choked on something." He offered me his drink. "Need to wet your whistle."

"Jean. Focus. You need to go charm some of these people so they'll buy a bust for their front entry or their house in the Hamptons." I had no clue what I was saying. I was from Brooklyn. "You need to create buzz—think big picture. It's not simply about sales."

"It is when the rent's due, boy-o, and the ex says that the kid needs braces."

Well, he had me there. Before I could respond, my ex passed by the door again—this time with one of the half-dressed waiters. Shep was decked out to party—black jeans and a cashmere V-neck sweater in vibrant sapphire blue. He had on a tooled silver belt and black cowboy boots, which were frankly ridiculous. He preferred being ridden. His platinum hair was nearly white in the down light—and that dick still had a drink in either hand. He glanced through the doorway. Eyes the color of caramel found Jean Luc, and then his gaze locked on to mine.

He had to go.

"If you'll excuse me. I need to find the caterer."

"Poppy? That's a hot piece of ass right there, I tell you what." He made a crude gesture with his hands at breast level as if he were dialing the knobs on some...well...on some woman's chest. I checked to see if anyone was photographing us. He was all about the big hand gestures tonight, which wasn't exactly what we needed for the papers. Jean winked at me conspiratorially. "She's got a set of tits on her I'd love to cast in bronze. If you hear me. Sweet mouthwatering nuggets. Perfectly proportioned. I thought you didn't swing that way."

"I swing howsoever I choose," I answered stiffly. "Now, I need to find the *caterer* to discuss the *canapés*. She's a friend. Please, spare me. And you need to find your shirt and go make nice. You look like the hired help. You need to impress these people."

"Are you not impressed?" He flexed with pride. Those nipple rings were bloody huge. Admittedly I was impressed. He laughed, his sloppy hair wavering around his head in an unruly, unkempt mass of gypsy curls. This time he managed to spill most of his gin on my good shoes. "Sure, Romano, but when you're done, you send our little friend this way." He winked.

"I just may."

My little friend. I considered her my dearest friend—the closest thing to a sister I had. After the final nail had been driven into the coffin of my relationship with Shep, she'd sworn to me that she'd keep our paths separate—and I had sworn to Poppy McNamara, launched debutante and Greenwich's most likely to land the cash cow, that she could fade into obscurity in the city. She wanted to be a caterer, much to the disapproval of her silver-spooned parents, and I promised to set her up. Over the past few years she'd managed pretty well. Christ, she made five times what I did these days because she cooked as good as she looked.

I pressed forward, dodging as guests snatched delicacies from the bare-chested waiters, swilled gin and laughed without restraint—I had to presume it wasn't at the artwork.

The gallery overflowed with friends, critics, buyers and freeloaders. I could barely move. Another photographer popped by, flash flashing in my eyes, and lumbered up the stairs. His bag smacked the wall, the clod. An ugly black smear marred the wall I'd painted early in the week.

Across the hall, the North Salon was even more crammed than the room I'd come from. Inside, Pappineau's sculptures stood on simple pedestals. Each bust was constructed from a bizarre and often shimmery jigsaw of men's accessories: shoe buckles, colorful condoms, odd tie clips, cuff links, watchbands. Anything Jean Luc could lay his nimble hands on, he'd used to create the heads. They were weirdly lifelike.

With discretion, I craned my neck, hoping to spy Shep. I sipped gin and watched as faces swirled by. Where was he? Not that I knew what to do once I found him. I couldn't toss him out of New York—well my cousin Joey would know someone who could, although that wasn't the done thing, particularly since Joey was retired from crime now and was in law school. But I could damn well toss Shep from the gallery without making a scene.

A man stepped out of the restroom in a Peter Falk overcoat and a rumpled beige dress shirt. His tie was plaid flannel, and by his stance I knew he was a cop. His hair was ungodly thick. He was a tall, masculine dude with peppered five o'clock shadow and a strong jaw. His coloring spoke of Italian heritage—irises and hair as dark as my own.

There were droplets of water clinging to him. Even his eyelashes were wet. Either he'd taken a quick rinse in the men's room sink, or he'd just come in. Evidently, the drizzle hadn't stopped. It was going to be a long ride back to Brooklyn tonight.

The door closer trapped the man's coat against the frame, and he struggled to turn around. I freed him from the door and offered my hand. "Caesar Romano. And you are?"

He peered at me without expression. "Detective Dan Green."

We shook, his long fingers wrapping around my hand in a grip that was warm and firm, but not bruising. He nodded, as if he knew who I was. He probably did if he was in the gallery. Maybe he had a fondness for Jean's work? Christ, wouldn't that be something? A fan. He didn't seem the type to appreciate more than an Escher print or a tapestry of dogs playing poker. Maybe I was being unfair.

I was paid to be friendly, so I strove to be so. "Are you enjoying the show?"

He gave me an odd smile. "Which one?"

"I'm sorry, I'm only aware of one show, and that's Jean Pappineau's."

"It's certainly...expensive."

"Ah. You're not a connoisseur. Did you see all the pieces? There's another level upstairs. You don't have to purchase. Most people are here to look and to have a good time," I croaked. My throat lost all wetness again. I needed some water. I put my gin on the hall table and grabbed a gallery brochure. Handing it to him, I saw that his hands weren't only large, they were crisscrossed with white scars. He wore a ring.

He saw me notice and slowly stuffed his hands into his overcoat pockets. We weighed each other for a moment, and then he nodded at the nearest sculpture—the bust of Justin Timberlake. It was life-sized and hobbled together with silver-plated watchbands, cuff links, buckles and laces. Justin's eyes were shimmery watch faces. Swatch Swiss. The placard read: *Time waits for no man.*

I'd seen them all, had typed the cards and laminated them myself. Even so, I had to work to keep a straight face.

"This is...interesting." He fought a losing battle to keep his own face straight.

I needed to tread carefully. "Yes. It is a conversation piece

17

at the very least."

We reflected wordlessly on JT as the waiters and the gallery guests swarmed the hall. The music seemed overly loud all of a sudden.

Brandon paraded past, striding into the kitchen, his ass swishing in tailored tux pants. He must be out of something at the bar. Detective Green surveyed him silently until the swinging door swung shut. "You always make your staff serve naked?"

"He's hardly naked. He's a model. I don't think Brandon, or any of the other men, will catch a chill wandering around semi-clothed. They're fairly seasoned. And it's a good gig for them because of the press. My caterer and I thought the naked chests of the models would counter balance the ornamental and stylized busts Pappineau created for this exhibit." Actually that was true.

The detective was anything but convinced. "It's not a health-code violation?"

"Is Hooters, Detective?"

He gave me a tight smile and let it go. "You're right. I guess I'd rather be at Hooters."

No kidding. "Well the gin here is free. If you'll excuse me, I need to speak with the caterer. Nice to have met you."

"Wait." He stopped me with a fast move, his spread hand landing a mere two inches from my chest. He was a big strapping guy and his action startled me. I froze, eyes wide. What the hell? We'd said everything that needed saying, what was his problem?

He cleared his throat, dropped his hand. "So. What exactly do you do here, Mr. Romano? I'm curious."

"Well, in a perfect world, I see to the caterer—which is what

I need to do right now," I said curtly. "My job is to keep everyone happy and out of trouble. Is there something I can help you with?"

"I'm just interested. You greet the guests by name, and you seem to be the one running the show."

He was watching me? Unsettled, I distanced myself by taking a step toward the kitchen. "Yes. That's often the case. My job is to make sure Peter looks good, that the pieces sell, the evening runs smoothly, and to know everyone here by name—except the gatecrashers, of course." I gave him an innocent look.

"I'm here with a friend," he said smoothly.

No way. He'd walked in for the free food. "Well. I hope you're both having a nice evening. If you'll excuse me, I really do need to check with the caterer."

"Is she a friend of yours? The Posh Nosh chick? Do you work with her frequently? I understand she's in and out of galleries all over the city."

I stilled at the too-inquisitive gaze of the frumpy detective. "Yes. Poppy and I went to school together." What a strange conversation. He was pumping me...like a cop. Maybe it wasn't that odd, but I was immediately defensive. "I can give you her card if you're planning a party, Detective." I dismissed him. "Have a good evening."

"I understand." He glanced around the packed hallway. "Maybe we could talk later this evening, if you're free?"

I blinked. Holy hell. The light dawned and suddenly his behavior made sense: the dude was hitting on me. This was a gallery first. I glanced down at the spiffy new blazer Joey had found for me in the garment district. I must look like a sure thing. I gave the cop a once-over beginning with his scuffed loafers, working my way up the surprisingly fit body beneath those rumpled clothes and ending with the strong lines of his face. Was he gay? He stared unflinchingly back, his gaze level. His eyes grew darker as the space between us narrowed and heat flooded my face. I couldn't decide who was acting more rudely inappropriate at that second.

A waiter flew through the door, and whatever passed between us evaporated. "Perhaps...uhm...another time." I extricated myself from the detective with alacrity.

"Sure." He handed me his card, which I took knowing I'd toss it, and then he nodded again and I walked away. I felt him watch me, my skin prickling as we parted. Hit on. At a show, no less. I'd be far more amused if Shep wasn't trolling the hallways like the ghost of lovers past.

"Caesar."

I swung around. My boss floated down the stairwell, his tux neat, his silver hair gelled into submission, his Gucci shoes freshly shined and reflective under the down lights. Suave, dapper, tall and trim, Peter was everything gentlemanly and correct. He had the usual hangers-on hanging on, and he was deep into his moment, as was the entourage. They nodded politely. I nodded back. It was all quite civil. We knew each other by day, but tonight I needed to mind my place. I was merely Peter's darkly attractive assistant.

"There you are."

As if I was the one sequestered on the plush second floor, surrounded by gushing pseudo celebrities and a bevy of beefy half-dressed waiters—no, I was the one manning the floor. Which was actually my job, so I adjusted my attitude appropriately. "Peter. Yes. You've found me. Clever of you."

"Now, Caesar, don't make a puss."

I swallowed and croaked, "How can I help you?"

"There are some interested people on the second floor. You

need to send Jean Luc upstairs."

"I don't think that's a good idea."

Peter came in close, and I forced myself not to rear back. Had he reapplied his cologne with a goddamn ladle? My sinuses clogged with sandalwood and...my nose tingled. Was that Noxzema?

Peter went on. "What a crowd. We'll be in the art section on Sunday, I'm sure. Peter Stuhlmann Gallery art show a bust."

"I don't think that's actually the headline we want."

He clapped me on the shoulder, and I took a breath through my mouth. I let him continue congratulating himself— pretty much an established pattern of his. "We've done it. I'd give myself a raise, but that's not necessary."

"You could always give me one."

"What's wrong with your voice? You sound like Colleen Dewhurst." The entourage tittered.

"I had an incident." I swallowed more gin. I needed to find a Perrier before I fell down. A waiter came by with a tray of chicken satay, which I declined. Peter took two. Armed with skewered poultry, he entered the North Salon brandishing his treats. He gave a hearty, "Ah-ha! There's the man of the hour."

I really needed to keep those two from making a scene. From the corner of my eye I noticed Detective Dan swiping a crab-stuffed mushroom cap from a silver tray. Then the kitchen door swung and I caught a glimpse of silver-blonde hair. *Poppy.* She was in the kitchen, where she damn well belonged. I spun and banged through the door.

Inside, the kitchen was a hive of activity. Waiters dumped glasses into the dishwasher and flew out of the swinging door brandishing refilled platters. Poppy frantically assembled hors d'oeuvres in decorative fantails on silver trays. Her platinum hair was neatly held in place by her customary headband—this one a soft periwinkle blue that matched both her dress and her eyes. In a white apron she looked deceptively innocent, like Alice in Wonderland.

Brandon stood with the fridge door open rifling for something. He dug out a Diet Coke. Poppy's assistant Rachel—I had no idea what she was doing, but it appeared she was hitting the warming oven with a wrench. She squawked. "Why won't this goddamn thing work?"

Poppy handed a tray off as another waiter came in and deposited an empty in the lineup. "I don't know, but you've got to figure it out."

Rachel blew out a breath and opened the oven door. "I told you we needed a new one. Did you listen? No." She turned the entire appliance around on its casters and contemplated the back thoughtfully. "Let's just serve all the hot stuff at once and then finish with dessert."

"Then get your ass over here and start loading trays. You may have to serve too."

"Well, I'll need to find some other shoes." We all stared at her stacked four-inch Mary Janes. "These are a bit tall."

I elbowed Brandon aside and grabbed a Perrier. "Poppy."

She didn't even pause. "Not fucking now, Ce, I'm busy. You're so lucky I love you, because this is insane. No more freebies. Unless you're stripping down to serve?" She stopped cold and shot me a cunning smile. "You know, you could. You're tight. Who doesn't like a good-looking paesan with a little chest hair? And that would be a huge help. The warmer is done for and all this food will be cold before we can feed the masses. You didn't tell me it was going to be a fucking crush."

The waiters were giving me a skeptical once-over. Rachel did as well. She eyed me cutely. Chesty and sweet, she reminded me of Betty Boop, more so when she opened her mouth. "Really? He seems scrawny. Take your shirt off, Ce. I wanna see your abs. We're having a crisis and this could lighten the mood."

"No. What the hell is going on, Poppy? Shep's here."

"You need to put the liquor down because he's not here. He's out celebrating. That pilot got picked up last week. Some...kid's show or some shit, and he and his people went clubbing. Can you either help or leave? Please? I'm not digging this. You're stressing me."

I took a sip of my drink and watched Miss Poppy. She did seem flustered. The waiters were staring between the two of us. Even Rachel went silent. "He's here. He's in the other room wandering around with Andre the hand model, and he's practically swimming in gin."

Poppy shrieked at the help, "Pick up a goddamn tray and get your tight asses back to work. I don't pay you to look pretty." They dove for the food and flew through the door. "Are there any more trays?"

"Poppy."

"What?"

"See if he's here. Text him and tell him to leave."

"Fine. I'll check. Rachel, load these. And you. Brandon. What the hell are you doing? Get the fuck out there to the bar."

"Just here for some limes, chief." Brandon industriously located a plastic bin from the refrigerator then skipped back out the door.

"He's a good egg, but I think he's getting too old for this thing anymore. He's forty-five."

"Poppy. Goddamn it," I snapped. "I can't concentrate with Shep wandering around. He's a distraction and he's macking on the help."

"Fine. He's not here, though. I'm telling you." She brushed her hands off on her apron, reached in to the pocket and found her tiny pink cell phone. "Just hold on and calm thyself down."

I stuffed a chunk of lime into my Perrier bottle and took a sip. It burned. Oh God. Maybe I *had* abraded my throat.

The door swung on its hinge again as another waiter flew in. From the door I could see Sheppard answering his text. He'd taken his sweater off. Apparently, he hadn't seen the need for an undershirt. "Oh my God. He's half naked."

My horror must have radiated from the kitchen. He glanced up and our eyes met. One corner of his mouth hitched, and he winked—like we were having some kind of private moment or an intimate joke. But there was nothing funny about this. Shep smiled as a slinky young woman slid her arm around his trim hips and the door closed.

"Oops," Poppy muttered. "Yeah. That's Shep, all right. What the *hell?*"

I flew out of the kitchen, the door banging against the freshly painted wall, my fists clenched, my ass clenched, and my jaw—you guessed it—*clenched*. I heard Poppy say, "Well that popped his fucking cork. Did you see that, Rach?"

Shep stood there waiting for me, smiling like a goon and nonchalantly sipping his gin. His chest was orange, but beautiful. Sculpted by a true artist—or paid for by Shep. He must have a personal trainer these days. That pissed me off more. I was living in my nana's guestroom eating Pop Tarts and my dad's pizza pie four days a week, and Shep McNamara had hit the big time. He'd landed the breakthrough role at twenty-eight. What was he doing here? No doubt rubbing my nose in his latest success.

My manly vigor went unnoticed by everyone except Rach

and Poppy. The hall on my end was remarkably empty. Not a good sign. Peter and Jean must be in the South Salon where, had the fire marshal been invited, we'd be running into a problem with room capacity. There were easily over a hundred people squished in that room, and more spilled into the hall behind Shep and into the North Salon. What the hell was going on? Maybe Jean Luc was offering an impromptu discourse on sculpture? Not likely.

I arrived ready to blast my ex, but behind him, Jean Pappineau wasn't lecturing unintelligibly about the integrity of his art.

Oh no.

Everyone in the room was topless. The men were at any rate. For many, this was a poorly conceived plan.

Shep waited for me to react to what I now saw was his vie for my attention—honest to God, why?—while, utterly distracted, I prayed no one had lost more clothing. Jesus. This could be a full-fledged disaster. The room was flashing with the white light of flash bulbs and the music was now much too loud and not at all appropriate for the event. Were we listening to...Biggie Smalls? Cringing, I searched for the detective. I wasn't sure if this constituted public indecency—technically Jean still had his skimpy black briefs on, and they couldn't begin to cover what God had quite unjustly been damned generous with.

I caught Dan Green's dark stare from across the room. He leaned against the far wall, his brawny arms folded across his equally brawny chest. His coat was gone, and in his left hand he held a colorless cocktail garnished with olives. His sole focus was on me—not Jean and his ass-hugging undershorts, not the shirtless guests or the equally bare waiters, and certainly not on the pumping bass or the free food. He was watching me with sharp-eyed intensity. His brow lifted and heat crawled up my neck. I'd have to wear this blazer more often.

"Ce. How are you?" Shep's hand came out to shake mine, and I smacked it away. I broke the cop's gaze and gave my full attention to the writhing crowd. I brushed past my ex-lover and threaded my way into the room.

"Shit," I muttered.

Jean Luc Pappineau hopped on top of the bar, swinging his hips obscenely. Andre the hand model gazed rapturously at that wagging package—Jean was hung, no doubt about it. The room was pulsing with grinding, half-naked art collectors. I scanned the room for Mallory Albright. She stood by the front window, clapping rhythmically along with the music, her head bobbing awkwardly. She smiled and watched Jean Luc with newfound interest. Thank heavens; at least she was enjoying my worst nightmare.

I'd tell her it was a happening.

"Caesar." An orange hand gripped my shoulder. I shrugged Shep off. His alcohol-soaked breath hit my face and my eyes watered. "Holy shit. He wasn't naked two minutes ago. Woo! Take it off, Papp."

"Shut up."

"Hey, you really know how to throw a party, Ce. You've changed. You look good."

I blinked. "You mean I've changed enough to look good?"

"No! No!" He gulped from his glass. How much had he drunk? "I mean, you're obviously in charge of this party, and it's wild and sort of out of character."

"It wasn't supposed to be wild, Sheppard. It was supposed to be a gallery opening. Pretty cut and dry. Hobnob—sell art."

"Well, I haven't seen this much gin since your Uncle Tino

opened that liquor store and supplied your cousin Tina's wedding. Remember that? That was a night."

Tino and Vito were my well-connected uncles. For them, family always came first.

"My Uncle Tino got this gin for me at cost. If you'll excuse me? I need to get Jean Luc down from the table before he shows us all his Prince Albert."

Shep laughed as if I'd made a joke. I should find my boss to see if we'd made any sales and calm everyone down and get these people the fuck out of here before we had a...a...*rave* or something. I didn't wait for Shep to say another word. I located Peter and made a beeline for his silver hair and half-naked groupies.

Shep disappeared into the crowd and when I looked back, he was gone—as was the mysterious Detective Green.

# Chapter Two:
# Trouble's a Brewin'

I took the subway to West 4th Street, stopping first at the bakery for a bear claw and a triple shot latte. I'd need all the chemical assistance I could get today. At ten a.m. on Saturday, I was slightly worse for wear. I could feel the gin leaching from my pores into my one and only cashmere sweater. It was fifty-nine degrees in New York, and the fog had risen, leaving the sidewalks damp. On Cornelia Street the trees were fuzzy, tipped with fresh red buds, and the morning seemed somewhat cheery. Spring, making its fashionably late appearance in New York, was almost in sight. It was about time.

I climbed the stone steps to the gallery and peered through the elegant leaded-glass door. Peter's building was a real gem. A former row house, the building was alive with tourist-attracting details: the curlicued wrought iron with pineapple-newel posts, the peaked roof and blond brickwork, and out front, of course, our discreet gilded sign—*Peter Stuhlmann Gallery*. Through the warped glass the hallway was dim, but any evidence of the insane revelry from the opening last night had been neatly cleared. Poppy and her stable of able-bodied, cash-poor, washed-up male models had done well.

I unlocked the locks and went inside. The salons were silent, everything in place, though the entire gallery felt hung over and exhausted. Naturally, it smelled like a distillery. At least we'd sold twelve busts. Some lucky orthodontist in Wilton would be paid, and it had only taken a few cases of discount gin. God willing, no one would reconsider in the light of day.

My finger hovered above the keypad of the alarm—the raised red light was disturbingly dark. Damn Peter. He'd left it disarmed again. I looked over my shoulder down the empty hall where the hardwood floors were a bit scuffed this morning. Peter was the last one to leave, sometime near midnight, and the moron had failed to keep his own property secure. I should call him and bitch, but he was at La Guardia catching a flight to Santa Fe. I bet he was still smashed.

I locked the door behind me. The building seemed safe enough, and I had plenty to do before eleven. I needed to call the delivery service and get these busts crated; I had paperwork to attend to and a resume to update. My boss was out of town for the next couple of days, schmoozing on his grandmother's dime. I was free to wrap up with Jean and get the gallery back in order.

A creak from overhead startled me. What the heck? I stared at the ceiling.

After we'd coaxed everyone back into their clothing and poured them into cabs, I'd checked the building, but...maybe Peter hadn't. He'd been fairly drunk, wavering in the hall telling me to go home.

*"You've done your work, now go home."*

*He had Rachel clinging to his arm in her stretched red polka-dot dress and those towering Mary Janes. Her cleavage strained against the confines of her bra, her lipstick was freshly applied, and I knew she was about to make another bad call. "Rachel, you wanna split a cab?" I threw her a lifeline.*

*"Nah. I'm good, Ce." She clutched Peter's arm and batted her*

*lashes.*

*Ever the gentleman, my slick boss smiled at her chest. "I'll have a cab bring you home, dear. Are you on the Upper East Side?"*

*She shook her head, curls bouncing around her pale face. "Staten Island."*

As if he had to ask?

So I left. And my boss hadn't set the alarm in his rush to sexually harass the help.

In the gallery, the silence was absolute. Maybe the wood flooring had expanded and made a pop. It was probably nothing.

I shrugged out of my jacket, charmed to see the back covered with white cat hair. If it had gotten on my sweater, I was going to have words with Nana. I picked at the hair and considered calling the alarm company, just in case Peter had set it, but...that was ridiculous. I was the only other person with the code and the gallery was fine. I stuck my jacket into the hall closet, and brushed away my concern with the lint and the cat dander.

The cavernous gallery was eerily gray. I flipped the lights and headed to my tiny office between the bathroom and the kitchen. First thing on my to-do list was to make more coffee.

I hadn't even turned the knob before another thump rattled the ceiling directly above my head. That was not my imagination. Could there really be an intruder? There wasn't much to steal. One would think they'd be more...covert...or selective. Maybe it was a mouse. "Hello?"

Screw it. I knew how to deal with this. My father taught me a thing or two. I marched back, grabbed an umbrella from the cloak closet—not as good as a Louisville Slugger but I could make do—and crept up the stairs on the balls of my feet,

30

retrieving my cell phone from the back pocket of my khakis.

I stopped on the landing and cocked my head, listening. It was ghostly quiet and overly warm. I let my eyes grow accustomed to the shadows. The décor upstairs featured sleek white walls and glossy blond wood. It was laid out more or less like the first floor. Where the kitchen was downstairs, Peter's office stood above, locked tight for the weekend.

I searched the hall. Halfway down, something shifted on the floor. Rat? Not possible. Maybe someone in the building had lost a cat? There were apartments on the two floors above us. Peter stored his private collection on the fifth floor, but that was only accessible through his office. I hoisted the umbrella and slunk forward, my sight narrowed on the moving mass.

The mass turned out to be feet. Big-toed, bare, square-knuckled feet. They stuck out from the bathroom doorway. They hadn't been there last night. I crept forward, umbrella raised. The toes wiggled, and this time a groan warbled from the men's room floor.

The foul scent of digested gin met me at the door. "Oh shit."

It was Shep, moaning and twitching. He lay sprawled naked across the white tile of the tiny powder room. I flipped the light switch, and he recoiled like some kind of night-dwelling rodent. He had a watchband wrapped around his dick and a morning beard covering his chin. That was it.

"Shep, what in the hell are you doing here?"

"Gah. Turn it off, man."

His skin was prickled with gooseflesh. I poked a toe into his thigh. "Wake up. You need to go."

He rolled his head toward the toilet, looking ill, though still more orange than anything else. Served him right. He'd passed out. Was this the life he led now? How the hell had he gotten in here? And where were his pants? "Shep. Get *up*."

I shook him, and he opened a bloodshot eye.

"No. Turn the light off. You're burning my retinas."

I hit the switch and put down the umbrella. I flipped the hall lights and soft beams filled the narrow space. In the front rooms, weak sunshine filtered in from the street. "Are you hurt?"

Shep mumbled, "Just my head."

Reluctant concern crept under my disgust. "Did you hit it?"

He moved his head and groaned again. I gave in and knelt down, ignoring his super spray-on tan and his rock-hard body long enough to see if he had a bump or a gash or a knock on his noggin. I'm sure that Mallory would have had a morbid tale of death by toilet to share, but I kept my mouth zipped.

Shep's hair trickled through my fingers, soft and a pure blond as pale as Poppy's. His breath was like a sewer. I backed away, sitting on my heels, and stared at his dick. What the hell had he done? "You're fine. Or close enough. You have a watchband on your penis. New form of play, Shep? I could call the cops, you know. I almost did."

"You would." He blinked a couple times and finally opened his eyes enough to focus. Then my words registered and he stared down at his limp cock. "How the hell did that get there?"

"Where are your clothes?" I refused to further examine the only thing he was wearing.

He slapped both hands over his crotch. "Jesus. Where are my clothes?"

He was still drunk. "Just wait here. I'll go see if I can find them." I soaked a paper towel and handed it to him. "Here. Wipe your face. You're green. And orange."

Shep tried to sit. He flopped to the floor almost immediately, saying with an audible swallow, "I think I'm going to be sick."

"Lovely." I left him to deal with his own discomfort and searched the second floor for his clothing.

The sound of my guest upchucking accompanied me as I went along my business. He puked in one of those deep-from-the-toes vomits that I well recalled from our nights in the dorm. Although he hadn't been known for excess. Not usually. He'd been all about keeping secrets and not losing control.

What the hell had he been thinking? And where had he hidden when Peter locked up? I peeked in the salons and the supply closet, as well as the lady's powder room, hoping to find his jeans—or at the very least, his underwear. Nada. I went downstairs and poked around, and finding nothing, I grabbed a tablecloth from the kitchen and headed back. Shep sat on the toilet lid with his head in his hands. His knees were pressed together, and a paper towel covered his privates. His new haircut was still unreasonably attractive.

"Ce?"

"Here. It's all I can find." I draped him in sixty inches of hemmed muslin. "Is there someone you can call to bring you some pants and...shoes?"

"I don't know. My agent maybe, but no one can know I'm here." He lifted his chin. His eyes were round, his version of imploring. I looked away. He was an actor and I'd seen this particular show before. My gaze fell on the watch he'd placed on the sink. Shep used his everyman voice, pleading with me. "I'm telling you. No one can know I'm here. I signed a huge contract and...I can't have any bad press or...any scandal."

"Mm-hm. Scandal? What do you mean?" That watch was familiar. "Is this yours?" I scooped it up. It was broken, obviously. The band was stiff with tiny pubic hairs...no...they were strands of dried glue.

"What? No. I don't know where that thing came from."

"Did you screw someone here in my place of work? Boy or girl?"

Silence.

"Or both?"

"I don't think so. I'm still...you know...I'm not doing that."

"Doing what? Boys? Girls?"

He cringed. "I'm seeing women." He lied to me with ease. I knew better. Also Poppy had told me otherwise. "Was there a chick here with nipple rings?" His expression turned hopeful. As if last night he'd become the straight man he pretended to be. He was an idiot. "I swear, I don't remember. I think I was with...a guy. Tall, no shirt? He had on a bow tie? What were you wearing?"

I gave him a frosty stare. "It wasn't me. You've just described every waiter here last night. And most of the guests. And Jean. You can't miss those things. What color hair?"

"She... He..." Shep looked pained, "...had...I don't know. It's all sort of fuzzy."

I clenched my teeth. "The hair or the memory? You know, *Sheppard,* for someone who needs to be *'careful'*..." I made exaggerated quotation marks with my fingers, "...you're missing the mark. There were photographers everywhere."

He buried his head in his hands. "I don't know what happened. I was celebrating. It's a fuck of a lot of money when a pilot gets picked up. Things got out of hand."

"Yes. Your being here at all is testament enough. And this conversation isn't getting you any clothing." I dialed Poppy. "Does Poppy have a key to your place?" Her phone rang and went straight to voice mail. "Call me right now," I barked into the phone.

"Yeah. But I don't want to deal with her."

I couldn't believe him. "That's too bad. You need to get dressed."

"We could call Estelle—my agent."

"Fine." I handed over my phone and left him tying a makeshift toga around his shoulder, his big feet naked on the cold tile. I could step around the corner to Urban Outfitters and buy some clearance jeans, but, goddamn him, I wasn't going to help. I had work to do. "There's mouthwash under the sink."

In principle, that was helping me, not Shep, because his breath could strip the varnish from the floor.

I went to the kitchen to brew a pot of coffee. As I swung back through the door, coffee burbling behind me, I realized where I'd seen that watch.

Justin Timberlake.

The featured piece from the collection—the one that graced the cover of the catalogue my Uncle Vito had printed for me at cost—was no longer perched on its display stand. How could I have missed that?

"*Sheppard.*"

I stood for a moment, scowling at the empty space above the pedestal, and then I bustled down the hall, breathing heavily. I searched every square foot of the gallery—the North Salon, the South, the men's room—I lapped the damn building in a haze of confusion. I didn't want to panic. There was a reasonable, plausible explanation for this. There had to be.

I dove into my office, the spindly desk naked except for the few business cards some of the guests had left and a neat stack of invoices written in Peter's elegant hand. No words uncovering the fate of JT. Only notes on which heads went where, how they were paid for, and what time to deliver. Donald Trump, Derek

Jeter, the Bloomberg, Rudy, Riley Albright, Howard Stern...all of them sold and accounted for. I tossed the notes in a pile and hyperventilated for ten seconds.

That head was worth fifteen thousand dollars.

Then I put the brakes on useless thinking and got pissed. I took the stairs two at a time and knocked into Shep.

"Hey. Slow down, man. I'm unwell."

"What the *fuck* did you do last night?"

He held his toga closed with his fist and grumbled, "I don't know. I thought we covered this ground already. Let's move on."

"Justin Timberlake is gone, genius, and you had a piece of him on your dick."

He struggled to make sense of that. "The watch? It was part of one of those statue things?"

"Yes, it was part of one of those statue things," I mimicked. "Did you break it? Obviously you did."

"I..." He hung his head in his hands. Was that true remorse or was he channeling Othello? "Can I get a drink of water?"

No. It was self-absorption. "Where is it? That thing is worth fifteen thousand dollars."

His head popped back up, his disbelief plain. "You can't be serious. Jean's stuff is that pricey? No way. Go Jean Luc."

"Where is it?"

"I don't know. Stop screaming. It's like nails on a blackboard, Caesar. Mellow out, man."

Hard-pressed not to shove him down the stairs, I bit my jaw so tightly my teeth creaked. I clomped back to my office to check the messages for the gallery. No text messages. I scrolled the gallery email on my cell and grappled with the facts. Could someone have paid cash and...brought it home in their own car? Oh dear God. But Peter would have said. He'd have left a
36

note right on my desk. Maybe the sculpture was with him? On its way to New Mexico? He was drunk last night, he could have done anything. I'd have to wait for Peter.

I stared out the tiny window facing the back alley, considering my options, which boiled down were: A) call the cops or B) call for Peter.

If I called the police, well that could be free publicity for the gallery, and after last night, we'd make every blog on the east coast—but Peter would flip, and we'd lose our credibility. Peter would want me to speak with him first. No question.

I drummed my fingers on the desk.

You know, I wasn't really the one responsible for the loss of Justin Timberlake. I could relax because none of this was my fault. I would have set the goddamn alarm. I could just point a finger at my boss, quit this place, and go work for the very lovely (and better paying) Mallory Albright. She'd take me under her wing. She might even allow me to occasionally have some creative input. Something other than dealing with overworked caterers and the fine-art transport guys from Long Island City— Peter could crate his own art and serve his own food. I'd be finally using my ninety thousand dollar education.

But Poppy's catering company would pay the price if indeed Shep had been fucked and then robbed by one of her staff. I couldn't do that to Poppy.

Outside my window, all was bright and shiny, though trash overflowed the small dumpster. Some insane impulse seized me. Maybe...maybe Shep and his new friend had broken JT and he was in the trash. I could fix it. Little hot glue, little floral wire, and no one would be the wiser. Dick Blick was only a few blocks away—art supplies just around the corner. How difficult could it be?

I unlatched the hardware keeping the back door safe and

walked away from the heady scent of coffee. I'd pour a cup when I was done. I'd certainly have earned it. Squinting, I stepped into the daylight.

A couple bums sat in the alley watching as I crossed to the reeking dumpster. Big and brown, it was full of germs and slime and vermin and disease, and I knew at once that I...I couldn't go in that thing. I wasn't cut out for dumpster diving.

"Hey." I waved to the bums. "I'll give you twenty bucks to find something for me in here."

"Fuck you, buddy. I ain't goin' in dere." A scruffy man in a red knit cap and a dirty buffalo plaid jacket laughed at me. He poked his friend. Man number two sat crouched in his own grimy coat. He nodded, peering up from his book. The two of them were side by side on a piece of filthy cardboard and watched me like I was the morning show. There was a bottle of my Uncle Tino's discount gin sitting between them. It was nearly empty.

I threw the lid open on the dumpster, and then I frowned at the cashmere sweater I'd gotten on markdown from Bloomingdale's. It was the single best article of clothing I owned, living on the peanuts that I did. I wasn't a clotheshorse, not really, but this was a V-neck in soft, unblemished, buttery yellow. I could not crawl into that rancid dumpster with this garment on. "Fifty bucks," I called. I didn't have fifty, but I'd bet the sweater that Shep did.

"Sixty." He blew his nose with his fingers and wiped his hand on his dirt-colored pants.

"Are you...are you *haggling* with me? I don't have sixty bucks."

"That's a nice sweater. Looks like cashmere."

I crossed my arms and narrowed my eyes. "I'm not trading. I'll give you fifty bucks to climb in here and see if there's a sculpture made of watches."

"Aw. No. It ain't in dere, man. I was in dere about ten minutes ago."

"You were already inside the dumpster?"

He nodded. "Had some of that cake from last night's orgy. And Joseph found some, uh, spirits."

"Did you see anyone leave that door?" I pointed to the steps and the wide-open door to the gallery kitchen.

"Couple of 'em. They was loading a van, and one guy had a big box. He drove off late."

Ah. Useful information. "The guy, what did he look like?"

"White guy. He didn't have no shirt on, and he had a bow tie."

Goddamn it. "Hair? How tall?"

"Oh. Tall, fit, and had a ball cap on. It was dark out. You still gonna give me fifty bucks?"

"You already were in the dumpster." I gave him ten anyway. It was my lunch money and subway fare. "What time did you see him?"

"Last night. Right, Joseph?"

Joseph, obviously the name of the bum reading a romance novel on his pallet of cardboard, nodded. "Ayup. Afta midnight, I reckon," he drawled. "Captain said he was nekkid."

"Nah. I said he was flauntin' himself."

Captain? The guy's name was Captain? "What kind of car?"

"Taxi. It was yellow and banged up."

I needed to call the police. I dialed Jean Luc instead. His phone went straight to voice mail. Then I dialed Peter. For him, I left a message. "Peter. I have a question about one of the pieces. Call me directly."

I ran back inside and was brought up short by the sight of Shep McNamara lounging in the kitchen, his strong hands gorgeously proportionate to the rest of him, his tablecloth draped effortlessly. He was sipping my coffee from my mug. He was as chiseled and compelling as Michelangelo's David. He was about as hairless as well. Although— "Why are you orange, Shep?"

"Estelle. She had me go to a shoot for the show—*Mr. Potter's Lullaby*—and they thought I was too pale." He smiled unselfconsciously. "I think it makes my hair look white."

"You look like an oversized Oompa Loompa."

He chuckled. "Thanks. Yeah it's supposed to fade in a couple days. It's bad, isn't it?"

I boiled over. "I need you to sober up and get out of here. This isn't a social visit. You need to remember who you were with. The guy in the alley said someone left here last night."

Shep ran a hand down his stomach, muscles rippling under muslin. He sipped more coffee and rested against the counter, striking his familiar *man having breakfast* pose. He'd employed it a time or twelve in cereal commercials. Not that I took notice. The terrible truth was that even orange, hung over, smelling of puke—he had that *it* quality which destined him for fame. I'd have bought anything he offered to sell me if I hadn't already sampled the lot.

"I don't know, Ce. But...you know I can't tell anyone I do guys. Not yet. I mean, at least not until the show is out, or after the first season."

"Ppfffft," I sputtered. I'd heard it all before. Not until Christmas; not until spring break; not until graduation; not until the second coming of Christ. "I need to call the police."

"What?" He set his cup down, his patina of charm dissolving. "No. No... Now let's not be hasty, Caesar."

"Hasty? This is my career on the line."

"Mine too."

"There was a cop here last night. I could call him. Detective Green." I recalled his too-interested gaze and that tight, knowing smile—but I'd tossed his card without a second thought. Perhaps that action had been premature.

"...because if you make that call, they'll write a report and my name will be in it and..."

"This is *not* only about you. We were robbed by whomever you hooked up with last night in my goddamn gallery. You selfish dick."

"You don't know that."

"Yes I do. Firsthand. You're a selfish dick." Before I beaned him with the coffeepot, my phone rang again. It was Poppy. "Poppy. Can you get over here and bring Shep some pants?"

"Where are you? What do you mean? Oh my effing God, did you sleep with him? Tell me you didn't do something that stupid." She was shrill. A deep voice rumbled something unintelligible behind her.

"Of course not. I'm not an idiot." Well, not anymore. Shep opened a cupboard door, rattling around for something. His color was high. He was smoldering a bright, angry orange. "He had sex with one of the patrons last night in the gallery and then he passed out. Whoever it was must have kindly stolen his clothes and left him."

Shep fumed. "Thanks a lot, man. Now she's going to be all over me. You got any Tylenol?"

I shook my head. "Where are you? Who's with you? Is that a man?"

"I'm taking a day off," she said carefully. Someone grumbled again in the background. Obviously Poppy had a secret.

"When did you decide to take time off?"

"This morning...look I'll be gone all weekend. I parked my car in the lot. Can you bring it back to my place? I don't want to pay for two days. Keys are in my desk."

"Poppy. One of the—"

Shep shook his head furiously at me. "Don't tell her."

I threw my hand up. "What?"

Poppy said, "Oh no. He's still there, isn't he?"

"Yes. Hence the call about the pants. Hang on."

Shep begged, "Please. Just wait. Don't tell her. Please."

"That's not good enough."

He grew more upset, losing his wide-eyed appeal. "Because this *will* lose me my job. I'll help you. I swear."

"Lie to Poppy? Just like old times, Shep?"

"I can't lose this gig. I need one day. I'll call every waiter who was here last night, okay? Give me the guest list. I promise to help you. I'll remember who it was, and then I'll find out what happened."

I couldn't believe I was considering it, but he was sweating, hung over, and more panicked than I was at the thought of Poppy or anyone else finding out he'd been part of this. "One day—but I'm going to have to tell my boss."

He nodded in relief. "If you have to call the cops, please, leave my name out of it."

"You need to grow up, Shep. You're twenty-eight years old." I spoke into the phone, "I'll bring your car home." I had her studio key on my ring for exactly this kind of emergency.

"Ce. I'm sorry about Shep. I had no idea he would come to the show. He's such an asshole."

"Yeah. I know."

"You're kidding me, though. Right? He's in the gallery buck naked?"

"In the kitchen as we speak. He's wearing a tablecloth. He's orange and he smells like puke."

Shep leaned back to watch me warily. His drape barely covered his thighs and was split to his armpit on the right side. He clutched the folds over his hip, but one wrong move and I'd see everything again. Big hairless deal.

Poppy whispered, "Can he hear me?"

"Not now he can't."

She hissed, "Sex in your workplace? Like he picked up someone in your place of business and banged that skank—wait, was it a chick? Not that it matters—and then he waited until you came to work to leave? Oh. That's just exactly like him. Exactly. That prick."

"Yes. Got it. Nutshell. Let's move on."

"I'm so, so sorry. I looked for him last night. I thought he left or I'd have thrown him out. It was just so fucking crazy with the clean up and the waiters and then I...packed everything and went home."

I could hear some mumbling again and Poppy covered the phone. There was some muffled talking and then, "I'm going to have to go in a sec."

"Wait. Did anything get broken last night?"

"Just that damn oven—maybe a couple glasses. Nothing major. Why? You break something?"

"Maybe. I'll talk to you later. Use a condom, Poppy dear." I hung up.

Shep offered a heartfelt, "Thank you."

"I'm not doing this for you, sweetheart, so save it. There's a coatroom by the front door. Go see what you can find." I poured my coffee, added two and a half sugars, and went back to my office. My space was puny, but at least there was a window. Daylight warmed my cheerful philodendron, its healthy leaves hanging in lush bunches nearly to the floor. I glanced around hopefully. Maybe an invoice had fallen under the bookshelf? Kneeling on the carpet, I checked for the fifth time. Shep came to stand in the doorway. He had on my jacket and it was too small. I wasn't a little guy, but like many men of my ethnicity, I wasn't reaching six feet in this lifetime.

I popped into my chair and my cell rang. It was Jean Luc. I swallowed a mouthful of coffee. "Hello?"

"Caesar."

"Jean. How are you this morning?" I wanted to scream, *Do you have the missing head of Justin Timberlake?* but I closed my eyes and prayed for a miracle.

"Good. Better, now that a river of cash will be flowing in my direction."

"Right. Congrats on a lucrative evening. Well done."

"Yeah, it was. So listen, Mallory and I spoke last night and she finally bent enough to put together a show. An evening of New York-themed contemporary artwork. *Relevance*, I think she said. Some shit like that. I need you to take two of the heads down to Parinella's—before you ship them, yeah?—and get them photographed."

"Me? That's not really in my job description—"

"Peter will call you. We had a powwow late last night. After you left."

He hadn't left a note. "Fine, which ones need to go?" I waited breathlessly for what I knew was coming. "We have stock photos from the printer, perhaps I can select—"

"No, she's got some curatorial vision. Those won't do."

"Of course she does. Dandy. Which ones? The Bloomberg? That defines regionalism."

"Nah. Not really interesting, is it? That was on commission. She wants the Timberlake."

"Uh. But...he's not from New York."

"Whatever. She's the boss. I just want to sell it."

I cleared my throat. Shep watched me from the doorway, taking in every word. "Mallory wants these?"

"Yeah. The Timberlake and the Trump. I'll have the transport guys come to crate everything. Are you there today?"

"No! No. Uh. I'll be busy tomorrow. We can pack them Wednesday morning first thing, if need be. I'm off Monday and Tuesday. Uhm. Did you take any with you last night? Did anyone take one home?" What a stupid question.

"I wish. Okay, listen, don't deliver the Trump to the lucky bastard who got it. You can sell the JT if anyone comes in and wants it, but they can't have it until after Mallory's done."

"Right-o." I sounded like Nana. "Will do. Any other sales that...I should...know about?" I hated stammering. It was an affliction I was prone to during times of stress.

"What's wrong with you? You still drunk? Great party, Caesar. Jesus Christ, man, you can throw me a party anytime. Maybe do my next wedding when the time comes."

Wedding planning? "I'm not actually doing that for a living—"

Jean Luc clicked off.

Hell. "Take my jacket off, Shep. Call Estelle and tell her you have thirty minutes to vacate because I need to leave."

"What crawled up your ass?"

Exasperated, I threw my hands in the air again. "Are you effing kidding me?"

"I love when you do that. The hand thing." He mimicked me. "Fahgettaboudit!"

"I do not do that."

The gallery line rang and we both stared at the phone. "Stuhlmann Gallery," I murmured, using no Italian hand gestures whatsoever—except for the one that employed my middle finger, which I waved at Shep.

"Caesar? It's Mallory Albright."

Of course it was. I dropped my hand. Sitting tall, I adopted Mallory's cultured waspy tone. "Good morning, Mallory. How are you today?"

"I'm very well, thank you. What an interesting evening. I had a lovely time. Have you spoken with Jean?"

"Yes. Just now, as a matter of fact. He said you'll need the Trump. You know, Mal"—here I went for my most conniving— "you should use the Son of Sam. It's very...compact. And it's regional and...the found pieces...particularly the buckles at the neck, are representative of New York justice overcoming—"

"No. The Timberlake. We'll raise the price and it'll sell. It's pivotal to the show. Did you use that kind of bullshit at Manhattanville? It won't work on me. I've heard it all."

I said meekly, "Whatever you'd like, naturally."

"I knew a girl who dated a cousin of that man—that Son of Sam man. It was all quite tragic."

"I'm sure it was." If Mallory's assistant Stephanie put in her notice by nine on Monday, maybe things would work out. I'd have a new job. I could find the bust myself or call for help. I thought again of Detective Dan Green. Maybe a private eye would be better. Did they even have those anymore? A dick. I looked at Shep. He raised his eyebrow and then went to the kitchen.

"You may meet me Wednesday morning. Ten thirty, yes? Steph's out this morning. I need the telephone number for your little caterer friend. Can you email that to me? I've misplaced it from the last time." Her carefully modulated tone turned crisp.

"Yes. Absolutely." Poppy had more work than she could handle, but whatever this woman wanted, she was getting if I had to cater it myself. Which, come to think of it, I could. "Whatever you need, Mal, you know that."

"Thank you." She hung up. I had time. I could find this thing. I opened my drawer and reached for a roll of Butter Rum Life Savers and the Pappineau catalogue. Justin Timberlake's strangely accurate face stared sexily back at me. I popped a Life Saver and grabbed a pen. I needed to make a list of everyone who had stayed after I left.

It wasn't much of a list: Jean Luc, Poppy, Peter, Rachel, Brandon, Andre...and Shep. Maybe a few of the other waiters. Mallory. I'd have to check.

"Who's Mal?" Shep reappeared in the doorway, snacking on a handful of grapes he'd clearly swiped from my refrigerator. He'd made a skirt out of his tablecloth and looked like an extra for *300*. He offered me a grape, smiling in that friendly, heartbreakingly handsome way of his.

It was an act. I knew better. I sucked on butter rum, my mouth twitched around the candy, and then something chirped from overhead. Shep and I froze, eyeing each other with renewed distrust. It was a cell phone. He dashed off, his skirt billowing. The chirping came again, faint but insistent, and I leaned back in my chair as Shep clambered up the stairs like a bull in a china shop. He was tall and loud and currently ungainly. I heard him scrabble around the banister and pound down the hall. The philodendron swung on its hook.

"*Where is it?*" he bellowed. Something skittered across the floor.

Why hadn't he called the phone to begin with, the moron? As it had so many times where he was concerned, suspicion gripped me. The phone stopped chirping, and I could hear the rough grumble of Shep speaking, but not make out his words. Beyond distrustful, a terrible resentment threatened to undo me. It also ruined the taste of my favorite candy. I swallowed hard, then snuck down the hallway to better eavesdrop.

"Yes. I know. Yes. I will. No. I didn't. I won't forget." He placated someone in a voice I remembered only too well.

I crept toward the stairs—but a knock at the front of the gallery caught me off guard. What now? Shep went utterly silent somewhere on the second floor, and I gritted my teeth. That man was as capable of hiding as my father was from his priest every Saturday at five.

I checked my appearance in the beveled mirror hanging above the naked podium where Justin Timberlake's head had once proudly rested. I looked good. My face was lean and strong, my chin smooth. No bear claw in my teeth. Eyes a little red, but the Visine was holding.

I went to the door. I saw the man who waited long before I reached the entrance. Detective Dan Green. How fortuitous. Somehow, he stood even taller and broader than he had last night. The morning sun gave his hair a deep, almost-red cast. He waited for me—in a mint-green polo and pair of opaque shades. The word *stalker* flitted briefly through my mind, but I dismissed it. He was here for something, and while I suspected part of the equation had to do with his apparent attraction to me, I'd lay money that he was working on a case.

I unlocked the door but blocked his entrance with a hand

high on the frame. "Good morning, Detective."

"Please. Call me Dan."

I felt the weight of Sheppard's fear bearing down on me. "Sure. Dan. How can I help you? We don't usually open until eleven."

He removed his shades and gave me a bland look. "It's eleven thirty."

I checked my watch. Actually, it was eleven thirty-eight. "Oh. Oh! Yes. C'mon in. Please."

Dan came in, his shoes thudding softly on the wood floor. He sniffed as he passed me, and his lips twitched into a funny, flat smile. He had a dimple. "What smells like candy?"

"Me. Life Saver. Butter rum." I followed him into the gallery. "So, Detective, is there something I can help you with?"

I took a surreptitious peek up the stairs, but Shep had disappeared. I couldn't blame him. I'd like to hide right now too.

Dan Green ignored my question. "Dan. Please. That was some party last night, Mr. Romano." His voice ricocheted through the sleepy stillness of the gallery. I needed to turn some music on to cushion the sound, but I already knew I wouldn't open the gallery today. I was bailing as soon as I got these people out of here. I was going to steal Poppy's car, call every waiter who'd been here last night and pinpoint exactly who'd slept with Shep. Maybe they all had, for all he remembered.

The man was still making small talk. "I was in the neighborhood. I thought I'd stop by to ask you a couple of questions."

Please. What did he take me for?

"Really? About?" His presence here...I could...possibly...use him. I glanced at him again. He was a cop, right? I mean, I wasn't sure if he was a menace or a savior, but I'd take either if it meant finding Justin Timberlake and keeping everyone happy and out of trouble. I cleared my throat and adopted my friendly management persona. "Were you quite taken by the show last night? Many were. Or is this part of some investigation?"

He gave a small, self-deprecating chuckle that set off alarm bells in my head. He was going to lie. Little frown lines appeared briefly, and then he smiled again. He seemed younger—maybe late thirties now. It was strange how transformed he looked today. I glanced down. No ring this morning.

"No. Not investigating. I'm curious about how this gallery operates. And about the artist, Jean Pappineau. You gave me a gallery brochure, but I was hoping to get a catalogue. I didn't pick one up last night. It got a bit crazy."

"It did. Better than Hooters, after all. So you need a catalogue. Yes, of course." This gallery? He was interested in us specifically? Good Lord. What the hell was going on now? The gallery line began to buzz. "Excuse me, Detect—*Dan*. Let me just get this call." I answered the phone in the hall. "Stuhlmann Gallery."

"*Who's that?*" Shep whispered from somewhere upstairs.

"May I help you?" My eyes flickered to the detective who stood respectfully at the doorway to the North Salon. I smiled stiffly.

"Is it a reporter or a photographer?" How could Shep achieve loudly demanding in a stage whisper? It was a credit to his acting ability. Dan Green could use some lessons from Shep, no question.

"No. Were you able to reach someone who can help you?" In other words: *Get dressed and help me.*

"What? No. Look, Ce, is that or isn't that a reporter or paparazzi with you right now?"

"Are you fucking kidding me? No." I hung up while the cop

gave me a curious look. "Wrong number."

"Sure."

Detective Dan wandered not so aimlessly around the South Salon, his keen eyes taking in every detail. The smell of gin was strong, but the floor was clear, and daylight lent us the dignity that Jean's bikini briefs had denied the place last night. I watched as Dan considered the bust of Derek Jeter. What evidence did he see that I couldn't? And what was his real reason for coming here? I didn't know whether to join him or not, so I stood in the hall wrestling with indecision. The detective didn't look so innocuous this morning. Nothing frumpy and fumbling about Detective Dan in the bright light of day. He looked powerful in his polo and jeans. He had motorcycle boots. How suspiciously butch. How shamefully appealing.

I waited—roasting in my sweater in the now-ovenlike building. Maybe this was a panic attack. I had to find the head, get Shep out of here, call the help, pick up Poppy's truck and land a new job. I needed to get out of that house with my grandmother.

Direction. This situation required direction. I pushed my sleeves up, rolled my shoulders and, mind set, I stepped toward the detective. He'd know how to help.

A noise from upstairs startled me once again. Shep came manfully down the steps, his skirt gone. Unbelievably, he was dressed. His platinum hair was a bit worse for wear, but he was more handsome even than a young Brad Pitt. His blue sweater, his two hundred dollar jeans, the snakeskin boots—it was universally unfair. At least he was orange, otherwise he'd have been overwhelming.

"Caesar." He smiled charismatically. He looked briefly to the man in the other room, saying for the benefit of our guest,

"Thank you so much for the use of your men's room."

"*Prego.*"

He then nodded to the detective. I had the strange sensation that they were sizing each other up. The detective wondering who Shep was, and Shep wondering if he'd sucked the guy's dick. Shep said heartily, "Well, I'm heading out now. Thanks for the coffee." He had the audacity to shake my hand and smack me on the shoulder. If he knuckle-punched me, I'd take him down.

"I'm just finishing, *Sheppard.* Why don't you wait for me in my office?" I bit out. He had better help me. "Where did you find—?"

He whispered, "Trash can. With my phone."

I checked his clothing. He had a paper towel stuck to the seat of his pants. I did not feel compelled to point that out.

Shep's hair fell forward slightly, and he reached to push it from his eyes.

Dan's eyes crinkled as he smiled in recognition. "Hey. You're the Wheaties guy. I've seen you on TV."

Shep, ever the attention whore, smiled. "And you are?" Maybe he knew this man for what he was—a cop. They could have met last night. Maybe the detective was the one who'd fucked and fled. They'd both disappeared at roughly the same time. I looked between them. Dan wasn't in awe of the burgeoning actor—which could confirm they'd been intimate if my recollection of an inebriated Shep with a half-flagged erection was anything to go by.

"Is that him?" I hissed between clenched teeth.

Shep all but shoved me out of the way, walking forward with his hand outstretched, eager to introduce himself to the quiet, watchful man with the scarred hands. I had to wonder what he made of our rude whispering and Shep's carroty skin tone.

The two exchanged names, and then Shep, hearing the word "detective", spun around to nail me with a wounded expression. "I thought we said no cops?"

Dan's eyes locked on mine and his bold brow went up. "I'm not here in any official capacity. I'm merely window shopping. Is there a problem?"

"No. Sheppard has an unnatural fear of authority figures— and men in uniform."

"What the hell are you talking about, Caesar?" He turned to Dan. "I played Detective Dan on television, you know? Hey. That's kind of cool. We're both Detective Dan." He chuckled and I was mortified for him. "I have no problem with police officers."

And then his phone rang and he stared at it. "I have to take this call. My agent, Estelle. Very important stuff. I'll be back." He stepped through the front door and I watched, slack-jawed, as he ran down the steps and hit the street. He hailed a cab, paper towel dangling from his backside.

"So what's the deal with him?"

My nose practically pressed to the window, we watched Shep yell into his cell phone and then hop into the cab. He never once looked back. "He's an actor."

"Yeah. So why's he orange?"

"He's an Oompa Loompa."

The detective chuckled. I could tell it was unwilling, but it slipped out nonetheless.

"So, Dan. How can I help you because, uh, something's come up and I...I...uh...need to run an errand."

He leaned back, the view on the street no longer of interest. "Is that typical? Aren't you the only one in the building?"

"Yes." How would he know that? "I'm here on the weekends alone unless Peter is in town."

"I see."

What did he see? "Well, I hope so," I said inanely and handed him a catalogue. Justin's Swatch eyes stared vapidly at us in full-blown Technicolor. "Is this everything?"

He rested against the doorway in no hurry to get moving. "Actually, I'd be interested in a tour, if you have time?"

"Tour?" I gulped. Jesus, he had it bad. "You know, we need to take a rain check on that. You could come by tomorrow." I didn't have time for whatever this guy was looking for.

Dan pushed off from the wall and pulled his shades back out of his pocket. Settling them on his straight nose, he said, "I'll do that. Tomorrow it is."

# Chapter Three:
# The Thick Plottens

I drove Poppy's delivery truck—her catering van was literally an old pink milk truck with *Pish Posh Nosh* emblazoned on the sides—back toward Brooklyn at half past twelve. She'd emptied her truck last night, presumably before she'd disappeared with her unknown guest, and abandoned it in the parking lot behind her catering café on 4th Street. I'd leave it at her apartment, but now I had commandeered it. I had errands to run. I also had her Rolodex. She might be upset with me, but it was often easier to ask for forgiveness than it was to ask for permission. She'd still love me tomorrow. Besides, I was only going to look up a few names.

I closed the gallery. It was as easy as getting rid of the intrepid detective, flipping the sign on the window, setting the alarm and giving the finger to the rest of the day. I needed to call every waiter on Poppy's pay list for last night, bring my nana for her weekly sojourn to the market, and—if at all possible—find Sheppard so I could throttle him with my bare hands. My cousin Joey was looking more and more appealing.

My cell phone rang—it was Peter finally calling from Santa Fe. I needed to tread lightly. He could be difficult. "Hello, Peter."

"Caesar. Why aren't you answering the main line? I've been calling since the plane touched down. We need a Saturday

LB Gregg

receptionist. I keep telling you that."

"We can't afford one. Why didn't you phone my cell earlier? I've...been...tied up. I need to ask you about the—"

"Shush. Listen to me. I need you to do something. You absolutely have to get this done."

I sighed. He never listened. What else was new? The light changed, and I stepped on the gas, hoping to make it before the light turned red. A cab behind me laid on his horn. "Sure and then we need to talk about the—"

"You need to go to my office, take the key from under the Rodin..." *it was a reproduction,* "...and unlock the storage facility. I'll wait. Tell me when you have it."

I was six blocks from the gallery and heading in the opposite direction. "All right." Shit. I looked around and, slowing, made a wide, illegal u-turn. It was awkward in the milk truck, and frankly insane in the city, but on Saturday the traffic was light. More horns tooted.

Peter yammered on in my ear. "What's all that noise?"

"It's coming from outside."

"You did a nice job last night. However, there's been an incident."

"Tell me about it," I mumbled. I stepped heavily on the gas, and the truck puttered along as I backtracked. I stalled him. "I need to check on...the...alarm first. Is something wrong? You know, the security system wasn't on this morning when I arrived. Peter, you have to set the alarm or we're going to lose our insurance."

Silence greeted that pronouncement.

"Hello?"

"I...thought I had set it. Are you sure?"

"The indicator light was dark. Yes. I'm positive. Listen. We

56

have a problem. One of the—"

"Have you been in my studio?" he asked frostily.

"Of course not." I had been in that area precisely three times in the past four years. "I respect the privacy of other people." Words that would come to haunt me later. "I've only been up there with you on those few occasions."

"Yes. Well. That's as it should be. I need you to go to the studio right now."

Christ. I zipped through another intersection, weaving almost drunkenly through the taxicabs. My stomach growled as I passed the McDonald's. "Can this wait ten minutes...fifteen tops? I'm starving."

"No. Absolutely not. I need you to do this right now. Are you with a client?"

I hated to lie. Hated it. "Er. Yes. I...need...I need...to finish...this. And have lunch. I feel weak. I'll call you right back."

"Five minutes. I don't have time to dally. I'm due for lunch in one hour with Donovan Treesprite—"

Who? "That can't really be his name. Is he Navajo?"

"He's Jewish. He's...had a transgression or something. You have five minutes. This is *serious*."

He disconnected, and I cut a cab off as I approached the pink light, sailing through the intersection at thirty miles per hour. I was four blocks away. Traffic grew heavier and pedestrians wandered the sidewalks happy to be free on this beautiful spring midday. On the corner, coming out of Denali's Deli, holding a sack of chips and slushie, was...was that Brandon? I did a double take. He had on a pair of jeans, a green Kermit the Frog T-shirt and a yellow cap. He was also tomato red—like Shep, only brighter. I yanked the wheel hard and parked in the bus stop. Brandon had a phone to his ear, his head cocked, and he appeared almost flash burned. He recognized the Posh Nosh van immediately and headed over. What should I do? I couldn't...accost the man on the street corner. Time was ticking down. I had four minutes to get to the gallery before Peter realized I'd ditched. Brandon peeked into the window of the truck curiously—hell, a lot of people were looking. He smiled when he saw me and nodded.

"Hey, buddy. You gotta move that truck. This ain't no parking space, asshole." There was a bang on the back door as someone whacked the vehicle with a fist. I put the truck into gear and made the universal sign of "hop in" to Brandon. His eyes widened and he nodded, climbing into the passenger seat.

"Hey, Caesar." Brandon smiled. "Good gig last night."

"Need a lift?" He wasn't just red; he was sort of slimy. I couldn't stop myself from blurting, "What the hell happened to your face? You were fine at eleven thirty last night."

"I had a procedure this morning. I just finished. I'm not getting any younger you know. I had a peel."

"A peel? Good lord. Why?" We jerked forward as I ground the transmission. I hated driving stick.

"To remove fine lines and wrinkles." Brandon rolled the window down and leaned his arm against the edge. His cap kept his hair from sticking to the Vaseline on his face. He was like a big puppy taking a drive. He chomped down on an apple chip and offered me one. "Why do you have Poppy's truck?"

"Oh. I'm borrowing it. She's away for the weekend."

"So what up, my brotha?" He laughed and flipped on the radio. I'd known Brandon for about a year and he was trustworthy, self-centered, liked to bang a lot of women, and was an extremely hardworking bartender. Like most of Poppy's employees, he was fast running out of modeling jobs and had to work like a dog to keep the cushy home he'd bought during his peak. Once upon a time, Brandon Wakefield had graced the cover of every romance book in the rack. He'd been Mr. Romance two years running. Then? He'd sold toothpaste and aftershave. Now? He was showing wear and mixing drinks five nights a week.

I cracked a smile. "Did you leave with Poppy last night?"

"Yeah, right after we broke everything down. Jerry and Andre and I stayed to clean. We all left about midnight. Why?"

"Just wondering. Someone lost a..." What? How the hell was I supposed to ask this? "...a watch. And I'm wondering who was around and...hey, you didn't find anything or see anyone take anything, did you?"

He smacked his lips on a chip. "Nope. Found a lot of empty glasses and olives on the floor. Saw a lot of beer bellies naked. Got turned down by my sure thing. That's about it. How's your throat?"

"Good. Your face looks bad. Shouldn't you be under sedation or something?" It was really hard to look at. I kept my eye on the road.

"Nah. This is my third medium-level peel. I've got a few more to go. They're a snap. You should get one, you look tired. Take ten years off."

"I'm twenty-eight, Brandon. I don't want to look underage."

"Sure you do. Don't guys dig that kind of thing? I can give you my doc's card." He lifted his lean ass off the seat and dug a business card from the back pocket of his Levi's. "Dr. Bronner. He's good. He does my Botox."

"I'll bear it in mind." I threw the card on the dash. "So nothing out of the ordinary last night?"

Brandon took a moment to sip his slushie. "Other than

Rachel hitting on Peter? No."

"Surely that wasn't unusual."

"Not really, but he's...ancient. I bet he can't even get it up. Oh. Shep being there, that was a surprise, yeah? He always looks good. For now. Hey, you can let me off here, right?"

"Do me a favor. If any of the other wait staff calls you and they've found a watch...or anything at all...could you let me know? Actually, could you have them call me directly?"

I pulled to the curb a block from the subway entrance, stopping traffic. Time was of the essence. Brandon hopped out, his face blazing in the sunshine. He tugged his cap lower. "Must be a nice watch," was all he said, and he shut the door.

I sped down the block and zipped into the alley, passing the two homeless men from earlier. Joseph had a piece of aluminum foil tucked into the neck of his shirt, trying to sun himself. I cut the engine and locked the doors. My phone rang as I hit the steps running. "Fuck, fuck, fuck!"

I punched the alarm code and raced up the stairs, gasping, "Peter."

"You were supposed to call me back. Are you upstairs yet?"

"I had to take a pit stop. It's been very brisk here...with foot traffic. Lots of people must have heard about the party. It's very busy." I cringed as lie after lie poured from my mouth. "Uhm. I haven't read the papers yet, did you see anything?"

"No. I'm in New Mexico."

Panting for breath on the second-floor landing, I twisted Peter's office door and— "Why's your door unlocked?"

He was quiet while I slipped inside. "I must have forgotten to lock it," he said stiffly. "Tell me when you're all the way upstairs."

"Sure." The office was bright since he'd also left the blinds wide open. The room was a pretentious, elegantly appointed place, as it should be. Original artwork hung on the walls—Peter's love of geometric abstraction and depth of color was evident in his workspace. These paintings were wild, bright and whimsical. Otherwise, the office was lean and spare and almost Swedish in its modernism. Sort of like Ikea, only far more expensive. Everything on the desk was shoved to one side, and a used condom lay forgotten on the Persian rug. Not at all like the fastidious Peter Stuhlmann. "It's very...messy in your office, Peter. Were you in here last night?"

"Yes, of course." He offered no other information, but the pungent tang of sex and gin and...some kind of stale fruit permeated the office. The fruit? Had to be cherry-flavored lube or condoms. Nasty things. Poor Rachel.

But I'd die before I picked up that condom.

"Okay. I'll call the cleaning service. I'm going in." I slid the key into the lock and stepped into the secret stairwell. It was dusty and private. Windows met the landing, allowing daylight to brighten the faded plaster. Directly below me, the new kitchen exited into the alley where the stairwell, once upon a time, had ended. That had been long ago when immigrant servants ran these floors carrying freshly pressed linens and tea on delicate trays. Not much different from my own job, actually.

The stair treads were scuffed, worn oak, the railing a deep walnut made smooth over the years by the chapped hands of domestics. I grabbed the rail and took the narrow set of steps two at a time to the next landing. Another large window let yellow light flood in. As the stairs twisted to the fourth floor landing, it grew dark, the air stale. Behind me illuminated dust motes floated lazily, but the locked entrance to Peter's secret lair waited in shadow. I was suddenly unnerved in the empty building—and sharply aware that in my haste, I may have forgotten to close the back door.

"Where are you?" Peter's voice boomed into my ear.

I jumped. "I'm just now at the door. Hang on."

"If I didn't know any better, I'd guess that you weren't in the gallery at all. I think you're in the Starbucks getting a caramel macchiato."

"Too many calories, I'm trying to stay fit." The bear claw had been more than enough. I scratched McDonald's off my list and thought happy thoughts about salad and another hour on the elliptical.

"It's a good goal. One can't be too careful. Look at that young lady last night—she's going to be plump."

"Rachel? She's a stacked little Betty. She'd look unhealthy if she were thinner."

"Oh, I was referring to your friend Poppy."

That startled a laugh right out of me. "You're crazy. Okay, I'm in. The door wasn't locked. I'm seeing a pattern here. What do you need?" I flipped the switch. The studio was in actuality his old apartment. He'd lived here during his younger years, before the trust fund had matured and he'd collected his fat paycheck. Each room housed different items from his ever-growing collection. Bizarre sculpture and large canvases he'd hoped would eventually become important. Many of these were boxed and stored, the climate controlled at a constant sixty-eight degrees.

"Go to the front room."

I'd never seen the front room. Nervously, I crept down the length of the central hallway toward the front door. I was freaking myself out. It was so deathly still up here, even with the huge windows gleaming midday sun, it was eerie. I passed the narrow galley kitchen and its adjoining dining room to my left, both filled with neatly organized boxes. There was a large room with a tiny brick fireplace to my right—the study. Built-in floor-to-ceiling shelves with locked glass cases were filled with orderly rows of rare books, another hobby of Peter's. Slipcovers draped the furnishings, and the floors were bare. The good rugs had been moved downstairs to carpet the gallery. Farther along the hall were a bathroom and two bedrooms. Compared to the hamster cage I'd rented that first year out of college, this place was a palace.

"Hey, the door is open." Why was I whispering? If anything, that made me more apprehensive.

"I was up there last night, during the party. I...took a friend on a tour. I think...someone followed me, or watched me. Maybe took the key."

"Are you kidding me?" Great. A lunatic could be hiding in the apartment and Peter had sent me with no weapon or backup or forewarning to his secret sex room. I felt like an indentured servant, and indignation threatened to choke me.

"Just go in for me. I need you to check the closet."

Jesus. It just got worse and worse. I touched the door, which naturally creaked in a high-pitched shriek that reverberated down the lonely corridor. I was sweating full out in my cashmere. I blotted my forehead with my sleeve. I was going to have to dry clean this sucker on Monday because I'd been sweating for two hours solid.

I pushed the door and walked in, only to rear back in horror. What the hell? *"Oh my God.* Peter!"

"You can't tell anyone."

It was terrible. I looked around madly, trying to take it all in at once. Everywhere—on every surface—the room was filled with...clowns. Knickknacks and kitsch snow globes, little music boxes with cleverly posed harlequins, ghastly porcelain figurines dressed in purple taffeta and red velvet. It seemed to all come from QVC. Garishly painted, a huge wood-crafted unicorn reared on its back legs by the window. Its hooves were varnished carnation pink. Here I was expecting a leather room or a sex slave chained to a post, but no—this was worse. Far worse.

"You can't tell anyone," he said again grimly. "I have been collecting since I was a boy."

"You paid for this crap?"

"Not...exactly."

"These are disgusting."

Over the simple wrought-iron bed hung a painting of Red Skelton's sad face. It was a gruesome thing of my worst nightmares.

"I know. I can't explain. It's a compulsion that seizes me and I...take them. Just ignore all that and go to the closet."

The white-faced painting watched me with forlorn eyes. I shuddered and opened the closet. "Just more clown shit, Peter, and a couple books. I'm so disappointed in you."

"I'm sure you have your own secrets. There's nothing else? You're sure?"

"A couple yearbooks—uh—Exeter nineteen sixty-eight, sixty-nine, sixty-seven. There's a book of poetry by Robert Louis Stevenson—someone took a crayon to it. That's everything."

Silence. "Anything on the floor?"

I checked. "Nothing but dust bunnies."

"Someone robbed us last night," he said with conviction.

Finally, we were getting somewhere. "Well, the alarm was off. Although how anyone could have known to go up here..."

"I was distracted for some time, and I'd been to the fifth floor earlier."

Who could have come up? Shep? Rachel? The waiters?

Jean? Actually, there were many possibilities. Anyone could have wandered in and gone unnoticed. Obviously Peter hadn't checked the building before he left. JT could have gone missing during the cleanup, as well as whatever carnival trinket Peter had lost.

"So...do you think anything else could have been stolen? Like one of the busts?"

"No. Frankly, I'd rather that had happened. At least they're insured."

It wasn't that easy. "We should call the police."

"No! No, no, no...let's not be hasty, Caesar. We can't have any blemish on the reputation of the gallery, and if it's let known that I didn't set the security system, the gallery would be in trouble."

Which was exactly what I'd thought.

He went on, "Someone from the party took something that belonged to me and is threatening to expose my secret."

I looked around the room. I didn't think it was any secret that Peter had questionable taste, but I held my tongue. "What was it? One of the busts?" I asked casually.

"Please attend. Why would I have you upstairs for that? And if a bust were missing, we'd know by now, wouldn't we? I bet I could cobble one of those hatchet jobs together in a half hour. This is *serious*."

Well that certainly put things into perspective for me. "Because one of the goddamn busts is missing."

He sputtered, "What? Why...? What are you...? Why the hell didn't you say so to begin with?"

"I was trying to. I knew you wouldn't want me to do anything until we spoke. I think we need to call the police."

"Police?" he squawked. "Does Jean Luc know?"

"No. But we need to address this. I think someone was here late and took it. Mallory says she needs it immediately. I'm not sure what you want me to do."

"Don't do anything. If it's the same person who took my...item...they want money. Just wait until you hear back from me. I'll speak with Jean, and you see what you can find there. Wait for me and don't let anyone in the gallery. You hear me, Caesar? I'll call you back. I need to think. I have to go meet with this Treefucker guy." He clicked off rudely, and I was alone in a roomful of clowns. Story of my life, really.

I locked the door and took the two flights of stairs at a clip, the day warm and all this exercise making me dizzy. I needed to eat something. I passed through Peter's office, which smelled like a lost night in Bangkok. I didn't look at the floor, just put the useless key in its hiding place and left.

Peter had barely reacted to the loss of the bust, which was pretty damn strange.

Something clattered on the back step. I cocked my ear to listen. Goddamn it. What now?

I crept down the stairs only to find the kitchen door closed and the front door shut tight and locked. The alarm was off, this time entirely my own fault, and on the fragile hall table next to the men's room was an ear. Justin Timberlake's ear. I stared dumbfounded. Had it been there earlier?

I slammed into the kitchen and yanked the back door open, nearly falling down the steps. Outside, the milk truck blocked the alley. The road was clear in either direction. Joseph sat on his pallet, tinfoil still tucked under his chin. His lids were shut, and I knew he was sleeping off the Uncle Tino free-gin binge. "Joseph."

I tapped his foot with the toe of my shoe. Nothing. I gave a start as Captain came around the side of the truck, zipping his pants. "What the hell are you doing?"

"Call of nature."

I ran to the side of Poppy's truck and nearly stepped in a puddle. "You pissed on the truck."

"Nah. Well, maybe a little. We had us some of deh gin dat was in deh dumpster," he said as if that excused him.

"You can't piss back here."

"Sure I can. Do it all de time."

I swallowed my revulsion. "Did you see anyone go in the back door? Just now?"

"Just you. You almost ran over my gud boots."

We both glanced down. His left shoe was stained with something wet. I stepped back, wondering if hepatitis could be airborne. "Look. If you guys are camped out here, could you...keep an eye on that back door? I'll give you...what do you like? Cannoli?"

"I like money. I also like scotch."

"No. I have cannoli. Have you ever had Rocco's?"

He swayed on his feet. "Dat sounds good. We're here. No one sees us. I'll write it all down."

I doubted that, but if they paid attention, maybe they'd be helpful.

# Chapter Four:
# The Circus of Despair

My nana isn't Italian. Just in case you're wondering. My brother inherited her Anglo looks and my father's Italian temperament, diction, vocation and wild hand gestures. I may appear to be a carbon copy of my old man thirty years ago, and be prone to gesturing, but I take after my mother's side of the family—The Coopers. New Yorkers for four generations, my grandfather was a mid-level accountant for thirty-eight years. After her husband died, Nana let loose. She quit smoking, took up Pilates and went yearly on a singles cruise to Cozumel. She enjoys a Cosmopolitan at five o'clock every night. She's seventy-six years old, and she's perfectly preserved. May Cooper looks a little like Carol Channing, but she acts a lot like Shirley MacLaine.

As part of her senior group, Nana dragged my brother and I to every show on Broadway—my mother to this day credits Saturday matinees with Nana and the ladies as the key to my homosexuality and my disastrous affair with "that actor". Paulie seems unaffected. My grandmother is far too interested in my personal business and regards my homosexuality as a dessert topping. I love her, but I need to be free.

I got back to the house at three thirty with Poppy's Rolodex, some leftover cake for Nana, and a cheeseburger Happy Meal—

which was all I could afford. My plan was to call everyone from last night. Instead, I sat at the kitchen table dipping my fries in ketchup, checking my email and examining the ear. I supposed we could rebuild Justin Timberlake. Peter said it could be done—how hard could it be?

Nana swept into the kitchen wearing a piped navy travel suit and a necklace of white balls the size of gumdrops. Her bracelet and earrings matched. She hustled over to see what I was doing. "That's an ear."

"Yes."

"What are you doing?"

"Working." Best to keep some things from Nana. "I brought you some of Poppy's special cake."

"Is it the raspberry cake with the chocolate ganache?"

"It is."

"Oh, that girl can cook." Nana's bracelet clattered, and the cat came running hoping for another meal. Bella purred, the little whale, but Nana ignored her. White hair coated her shin. "We need to go to the store, pumpkin. I need you to carry my bags. I think I may have strained my groin at Pilates this morning."

"You're fine, Nan. You say that every week."

"We'll stop at Rocco's for dinner. Ellie said she hasn't seen you all week."

Ellie is my mother—also not much of a Romano, although she made an effort. Rocco Romano is my father and his Italian eatery, nestled in the old neighborhood, was the family cash cow.

"Can it wait?" This thing was so peculiar, the way it was put together. It was extremely complex. "Nana, can I borrow your tweezers? Mine are downstairs."

She lifted a bleached brow and pursed her lips. "Sure thing." Still ignoring the cat, she went to retrieve her tweezers for me.

I checked my mail while I had the computer running. I had thirty-four emails regarding the party. I began to sift through them. Most of them said thank you or were forwarding a review. I skipped those for now. There were a few photos of Jean, Peter, one of me looking damn fine in my new blazer, and one of the crowd, many of whom were shirtless. Mallory and the detective were side by side at the bar, fully attired. They had the same color hair.

Nana interrupted, handing me tweezers. "Did you ever see the movie *Blue Velvet*, pumpkin? That ear reminds me of Dennis Hopper."

"It reminds me of Van Gogh."

"Or that Getty boy. They held him ransom and sent his ear. It was ghastly. And so public."

I stared at Nana, who as usual was right on the money. "Do you have a shopping list? I could go for you."

"I need things that have nothing to do with you, sunshine. Lady products. I don't want to tip my hand and reveal any beauty secrets. I just need you to look buff and pull the Winnie Wagon."

I sighed and studied the ear. It was made of interwoven chinks from a silver-plated watchband; they were adhered to some kind of fabric. "What do you think this is?" I turned it over. The bottom was stretchy and shiny.

"Umbrella fabric. It's Burberry."

"What? How can you know that? Like, within two seconds?"

"I have that umbrella. Well, the knock off from Canal Street. See the color and the cross-section? It's small—but it's

Burberry. That really makes a statement, doesn't it? That someone would cut a two hundred dollar umbrella. Very wasteful."

"You're right." Why hadn't I seen that detail? Maybe Jean had more depth than he let on. His satirical look at power and money was either going to be his claim to fame or cause him financial ruin. I shoved the photo away. "All right. I'll take you, and we'll go to dinner at Rocco's, but Mom will have to walk you back. I have some things to do." Like buy a glue gun and some floral wire without Nana's interference. I glanced at the ear again. Maybe I'd pick up some fine-tipped markers as well.

She nearly leered. "Does it involve a man? Let me just fix my lipstick and grab my good handbag. Oh, and I have a circular I need to take as well."

"Great."

We walked into the restaurant at seven thirty. I blinked in disbelief. Shep McNamara sat at the best table in the house, a bleached-out preppie man in a Vineyard Vines tie on his right, and an older woman with jet black hair and yellow teeth at his left. Even from the door, I knew it was his agent Estelle. She was loud and her crass laughter carried across the restaurant. She had a boiled wool jacket that screamed money and chunky gold jewelry that begged to be stolen. The three were clearly finishing a business dinner. Shep had a half-eaten cannoli in front of him.

"Shit."

Nana smacked my arm. "Mind your manners. Oh! Isn't that your college roommate? What's wrong with his face?"

Nana beamed and waved. Shep, seeing us at the door, flushed scarlet. He nearly matched the restaurant décor. He was still dapper and darling, yet underneath I knew he was frayed around the edges. Actually, he was wide-eyed with panic. Three times I'd seen him in twenty-four hours. This was insane.

My brother Paulie, blond as a Swede, came bustling up wiping his hands on his apron. "If it ain't the art fag come to pay his respects to the family."

"Nobody died, Paulie—I've come for veal scallopini. Tell Pop."

Paulie bent down from his great height and kissed our grandmother on her powdered cheek. Nana patted him absently and hustled over to Shep's table. "Sheppard! The big star. I saw you on *Days* and in that Wheaties commercial. How are you? I tell everyone in the Altar Guild that you and Caesar were—"

"Mrs. Cooper!" Shep jumped to his feet, scraping his chair and nearly knocking his espresso off the table. The demitasse spoon clacked on its little dish. He kissed her cheek soundly. "Roommates. Yes. Three years."

He nodded at me—suddenly so staunchly heterosexual I'd have set him up with my own sister if I'd had one.

"Caesar Romano, Mrs. Cooper, let me introduce you to my agent, Estelle Rosenstein. And the executive producer for my new show—this is Chad Schumacher. He's from Darien. He and my parents went to Choate together back in the seventies."

Gag. Pretentious *and* preppy. I nodded and made nice with country-club man. Nana, no fool, zipped her trap. Estelle Rosenstein flung her hand across the table and shook my entire arm with enthusiasm. Did she know who I was? I slid a look at Shep. "What a happy coincidence," I said through clenched teeth.

Shep nodded, grinned, laughed and basically jumped through every hoop. He'd have rung a bell and barked, I knew, if it meant fame. Chad sat quiet and observant. I smiled cautiously at him. He was a homophobe of the first order, I could almost smell it.

"Shep here is our new Mr. Potter." Chad's eyes were glowing blue. He had the look of a zealot.

"Mr. Potter." Nana turned to me. "That's the new show, Caesar. I TiVo'd the pilot for us."

"What? I didn't know that." God.

Shep turned a curious melon color. I guess he blanched. It was difficult to tell under the tan. He licked his lips. "Yes. We're just discussing it now. *Mr. Potter's Lullaby*—"

"About that name..." Nana shuddered and said in all innocence, "...I hate to be a prude, but it does sound unseemly."

I nodded. "Yeah. Like story hour for pedophiles."

Nana snorted indelicately. I loved her, plain and simple.

Shep shook his head at me desperately. He struggled to find the right words. "Well. It's a family show for...people...about making good choices. It's based on the book, *Mr. Potter's Lullaby?*"

"Was on the bestseller list for inspirational fiction. Six weeks running," Schumacher said, as if he'd written the book himself.

Shep offered weakly, "It's like *Seventh Heaven* meets...uhm... It'll appeal to typical American families. That's the target demographic."

"Sounds fascinating," I said politely. Actually, it sounded suspiciously middle-American. "Any gunfights? Car chases? Strapping young Scotsmen in kilts? I like those."

Chad's laser-like eyes flashed in annoyance. "It's a show that centers on traditional values."

"So, that would be a no to the kilts then? That's a real shame." I shook my head sadly. Nana grabbed my elbow and pinched me hard. "Ow. Uh. That sounds like just the thing this country needs."

My father saved us all from a scene. "Caesar!" He kissed my cheek and I let him. "You cumma back to the kitchen and pack uppa some nice cannoli for later." His accent was ridiculous. I let it slide, but hear this now: the man is third-generation American.

"Yes, Pop. I will."

"Your momma, she wants you to cumma into de kitchen. She's a working, yes?"

I told him to knock it off, but nicely. "*Smettila!*" My old man winked and I smiled back. He was working the table for a fat check.

I was unsurprised when Shep nudged my foot under the table.

"If you'll all pardon me. Mr. Romano. Ms. Cooper." He wiped his mouth neatly and placed his napkin on the table, then he fled to the men's room like his pants were on fire.

"I'll go back and see Mom now." I nodded to Estelle and rudely ignored the Nazi. I didn't play that game. I settled Nan in a booth near the kitchen. Pop went to make her a Cosmo.

I went directly into the men's room, just like old times with Shep, hiding from the public. I detested him. But I couldn't out him. I'd leave that for the press, because eventually the truth would tell, and Mr. Potter was in for a rainbow-colored surprise.

Shep grabbed my arm. "I'm sorry. Estelle read about this place in the Times, and we've had this dinner planned with Chad, but I had no idea we were coming here. I am as horrified as you are. I keep wondering if your dad is going to say something, or Paulie, and then you walked in. Don't act too gay."

"I don't act gay, Shep. I am gay. It's a beautiful thing to live your life in the open." Most of the time. Especially after payday. "Stop whining and tell me something new. Any luck? Did you remember anything?"

He shook his fabulous hair. Anxiety wrinkled his masculine brow, and I struggled not to feel sorry for him. Damn actor. "No. But...you need to see this." He whipped out his iPhone—an item that was entirely beyond my price range, FYI—and the next thing I knew we were watching amateur porn. I reared back, shaking free of his hold.

"What the hell is this?" It was Shep getting his face plowed by someone filming at an odd angle with a cell phone. The quality was beyond poor. "Is this supposed to impress me? I've seen you give head before, in this very bathroom."

"Ssshhh!" As if the producer had his ear to the door. Shep's hand shook. "It was in my email. I don't know who it's from, but, Caesar, whoever it is wants something from me. It's a threat."

I reluctantly watched the phone. "There's a lot of that going on. Someone left a piece of that sculpture today—and Peter had an incident as well. You don't remember anything?" He played the video again. Shep was so wasted, he was placid. My stomach turned. "This is horrible."

"I know." His eyes welled with tears, and I awkwardly patted his shoulder. It was strange to comfort him, but I genuinely felt terrible. He mumbled, "I'm going to lose everything." I squeezed his shoulder and he choked. I gave him a minute to regain his composure. Not a show this time. I knew the real thing when I saw it. "He wants money."

"Don't they all? How much?" This was so curious.

"It's the stupidest thing. He only wants eight hundred and ninety-seven dollars. And sixty-eight cents. It's insane. He's threatening my entire career over nothing." He pocketed his phone and glanced at himself in the mirror. He quickly checked his teeth.

"That's not nothing to me." I didn't have fifty dollars in cash, and my credit cards were groaning from overexertion. "He's bluffing. You need to call the police. This is vile."

"I can't. I just...I can't. I'm seeing someone...and my pilot was picked up. Do you understand how important this is?"

I nodded. Of course I did. "If you're involved with someone, that's even more reason." I kept myself from asking who he was seeing...but I wondered if some ingénue was waiting in the wings. "You do what you need to. We need to go back out there. Call me later."

"Yeah. Thanks." And then Shep did the unthinkable. He pulled me into his arms, hugging me quick, tight, like we were in some kind of Hollywood bromance. His cologne was the same, as was his shampoo. Christ, even his fabric softener—it all smelled comfortably like the past. Clean, like mountain air. Like a nice virginal straight college boy from Greenwich desperate not to be a homosexual and eager to experience the world.

It was a snug and private moment, the clatter of the restaurant seemingly far off. I felt his breath against my ear. The last time we'd been sequestered in this place, he'd been on his knees, begging me to let him get me off quick. He'd always been filled with surprisingly naughty fantasies. That one had been particularly exciting—with my parents only a few scant feet beyond the door.

Shep gave me a slap on the back and shoved me away. "Gotta go. Thanks, Ce."

The door snapped shut in his rush to get away from me. I sighed and went to join my grandmother, who was sipping on a very large Cosmo. A maraschino cherry stem was tied on her napkin. I knew she hadn't done that with her fingers.

She started in on me before I unfolded my napkin. "He looks good, Caesar, but when's he going to turn into an honest man?"

"I'm not holding my breath. Don't start with me. I'm not getting involved."

"From your mouth to God's ears."

I gritted my teeth and said slowly, "Let's just have our dinner."

"Fine."

I nodded. "Did you really TiVo that show? You never said."

"Yes I did, puss. I thought we could make popcorn and throw it at the television."

Paulie stopped by with a glass of Chianti for me and an antipasto for Nana and I to share. I snapped at him, flinging my hands wildly. "Why'd you let them in here?"

"Whoooo hoooo. Like I can do anythin' about it? I can't not let him in the door." He tossed a white towel over his shoulder and leaned a hand on the back of the booth. The vinyl creaked.

"You could have been full. No reservation. Anything." It would have worked. It was Saturday night and Rocco's was packed, every booth and table filled.

"Nah. They had reservations under another name. I had no idea he was gonna be here. Besides, Pop loves when celebrities come in."

That threw me. I was just going to have to adapt to Sheppard "Easy Mac" McNamara's fame. And this behavior was true of my pop, and admittedly good for business. I sighed. "Fine. But next time, warn me. You knew I was coming in."

Paulie nodded. "Okay, okay. Don't have a stroke. Hey, he's

77

gonna have a picture made of them two—Shep said he'd sign it so as we can hang it at the register, next to the Al Pacino and the Patti LuPone."

"Great." We watched as Estelle, Shep and the Evil One finished their coffee. Shep sent me one last long look as he went to the door. He mouthed *call me*.

"What's he want? You're not going to call, are you?" Nana's fork stopped mid bite, a slice of prosciutto dangling from the tines. "What a wimp."

"I should have Joey run him out of town." It slipped from my lips before I could stop myself.

"He'd do it, no question. Look out, paesan. Here comes Ma." Paulie scampered away as my blonde and dainty mother slid into the booth clutching a half-full martini glass. She kissed my cheek, and I smiled at the scent of Oil of Olay and oregano.

"What's that actor doing back here? Rocco likes the publicity, but me? Not so much."

"I know. I'm sorry. I have no control over these things."

My mother sniffed. "He's a nice boy, I guess, but did you see that television show? Horrible. He plays a missionary in Appalachia."

"You've got to be kidding. Why do they need missionaries there?"

"Apparently they require a man in tight pants to deliver awkward messages. I'm not sure. I fell asleep."

Nana drank her Cosmo. "You mark my words: that Chip man is out of his mind."

"Chad."

"Same difference."

An hour later, my belly full of veal scallopini and my head

stuffed with gossip, I crossed the narrow street to Poppy's pink van. I would have missed the man entirely if he hadn't met my eye. I wasn't pleased. It was Detective Dan, my own personal stalker, with a smoldering cigarette between his fingertips. He had on a soft leather jacket and a Yankee's cap low on his head, his black hair almost hidden. He blended into his surroundings seamlessly. He'd done that three times in the last twenty-four hours, and now I knew what was going on with the chameleon-like detective, and it wasn't a sudden interest in hooking up with yours truly. "You're following me?"

"Maybe." He took a drag of his cigarette. He'd gone from frumpy and unassuming last night, to powerful and clean-cut this morning, to dangerous and a little unnerving.

No ring again. "What the hell is going on?"

"We need to talk."

"Here?" The night was cool and the sidewalk dark on this side of the street. All along the block people were busy, returning from dinner or the movies, or heading out for the night. I gave him an exasperated sigh. "Look. I need to go get some art supplies. If you want to talk, climb in, we can have a powwow in the truck. I have things to do."

That took the wind right out of his sails. He shook his head in confusion. "Art supplies? Are you a painter? It's Saturday night. Don't you have a...date or a club or something to go to?"

"Me? Obviously you haven't been following me long, Detective. Other than the gallery and Rocco's with my Nan on Saturday night, I have no life. And no, I'm no artist."

He dropped his cigarette, crushing it under his boot. "That's a shame. Sure. Supplies. Maybe I can pick up a video game."

I unlocked the truck. "Hop in."

"Wait. Don't you even see that there's something on your

79

windshield?" I looked and sure enough, there was a small white envelope tucked beneath the windshield wiper on the passenger side. It was rumpled.

I glared at him. "You put that there."

"I didn't. I followed you, but I was inside until five minutes ago."

"Inside Rocco's? Not possible. I would have seen you." I yanked the envelope; the wiper hit the glass with a *snap*.

"Yeah. In the bar. Your family seems nice. Paulie said that he and Donna are trying to have a family. You know, that thing could have been on the truck all day. Look at it."

"You were speaking with my *family*? What the hell are you doing nosing into my life?" I climbed in and slammed the door. He climbed cautiously into the passenger seat. I took a deep breath and stuck the key in the ignition.

Then I wheezed. Realization hit. Could he be— "Oh my God. It's you, isn't it? You stole the bust. You're the one who fucked Shep—"

He held his hands up in some mockery of innocence. "No. Calm down. No."

"*You were in the clown room.*"

I'll remember this part forever because, in my race toward the wrong conclusion, I turned to face him, both my hands flying with typical Romano flair. I let go of the clutch a hair quicker than I should have and the truck jerked. I fell abruptly off the seat, sideways. He must have gotten the wrong impression. He reacted as if I were on the attack. I mean, the man was about six-foot-four, and I'm five-ten in my best shoes. Why in the world would I attack? I swear it was an innocent move, but as I lurched over the seat, he grabbed my flailing fist, swinging me around and twisting my arm painfully behind my back. It must be a cop reflex—man, he was fast.

I thrashed. "Ow! What the hell? Let me go." My leg came down on the gear shift, and like that I was tangled. I shook my pant leg, trying to get free. In the process, I knocked the shifter into neutral. The truck rocked briefly, and then it lurched down the sloped pavement. I was wrestling with the detective, all but sitting on his lap, when I noticed we were picking up speed.

"Would you just calm down, Romano?" He grappled with my wrist.

"Shit! Let me go. We're moving."

He looked out the window. "Why isn't the parking brake on?"

"I don't know. I'm not much of a driver. I'm a New Yorker." I straddled his leg the wrong way and managed to grab the wheel as he let go of my arm. We coasted through the intersection. Cutting hard to the right, I scrambled to reach the brake, but my pant leg was caught and I couldn't get back into my seat. I was sitting on his knee when we hit the curb, bumping onto the sidewalk.

"What the hell are you doing? Get off me."

"I'm stuck."

Poppy's top-heavy milk truck bumbled down the tiny incline. Pedestrians jumped out of the way. I wailed on the horn. Dan pushed and prodded and finally squirmed out from under me, calling me rude names and swearing.

"My leg is trapped on the gearshift, asshole." It was tunneled up my pant leg and I had somehow twisted around. My other cuff appeared to be trapped on a hook under the seat. I was too busy steering to free my damn pants.

Dan slammed on the brake, and I flew into the windshield. My temple slapped the glass. "Ow!"

"You are a fucking menace!" he screamed. "What the hell is

the matter with you?"

"Me? You're the one following me. Who are you? Did you have sex with Shep?"

"Shep? The actor? Newsflash—he's straight."

"And you call yourself a detective? Newsflash—he's gay. He's queer. He sucks dick in dark closets for sport."

Oh my God. Dan sat gaping at me. I snapped my jaw shut. I quietly freed my pants and took a deep breath.

Someone rapped on the window and we both jumped. Dan glared out the window, mumbling, "Jesus fucking H. Christ on a goddamn fucking crutch."

"Oh. That's helpful," I snipped. I rolled the window down. A police officer stared patiently into the vehicle.

"License and registration please."

"Don't ask me," I said. "He's driving."

Dan gave me a look—both comical and terrifying—and I was glad there was law enforcement present. His gaze moved reluctantly to the cop. "Evening, Officer."

I expected them to do some kind of secret handshake, but when Dan opened the door, the officer nailed him in the beam of his flashlight. "Remain in the vehicle."

"He's a police officer." I read the man's nametag. "Officer O'Brien."

Dan groaned and slid down in his seat. His hat sank over his eyes. He covered his face with his hand. "No, Caesar. Not anymore."

My temple throbbed as I whipped around. "What do you mean? Who are you?"

O'Brien said, "Is there a problem here?"

"Yes, there's a problem here. A strange man is driving my

best friend's car."

The cop's stare intensified and Dan said to me, "Could you please just shut up? You're making this worse."

"Worse? How can I make this worse?"

"I need you to step out of the vehicle, sir."

"Yes. Step out of my vehicle." Who in God's name was this guy? Why was he impersonating a police officer?

"You are not helping." Dan climbed out of the truck while I riffled through Poppy's glove compartment searching for her registration and insurance. Her papers were a mess. It took five minutes, but when Dan got back into the driver's seat, he gave me a death glare. "Do not say a single word until we get off this sidewalk, you got that?"

"Doesn't he need the paperwork?"

He clenched his jaw and then bounced over the curb; the truck lurched like a drunk. We eased into traffic and headed south, puttering along merrily. I left the radio off. I let Dan sit for a couple minutes, no doubt trying to regain his composure, and watched as the blocks swept by. He took the onramp to 278. We were leaving Brooklyn. I broke the silence. "So. What? You're taking me to Staten Island to dump my body in a landfill?"

"No," he grouched. "I'm going back home. I've only been watching you for two days and...you screwed things up by not taking the subway. I knew better. Serves me right."

"That means you're really following me?"

"Yeah." I watched him in the yellow glow of the passing streetlights. He had a strong face. The bill of his ball cap hid his eyes, but his jaw was bold, his mouth firm, his nose straight. He was scruffy with his evening beard. All in all, he was far better looking than I'd given him credit for. I guess this meant his interest in me was purely professional. Why was I disappointed?

He slid a look at me, then his eyes went back to the road. "You want gum?" How weird was that? He found a pack in his pocket and offered me a piece. I took it and sniffed it first, which made him smile. "It's fine. Eat it."

"Thank you." It was mint. Nice. I froze. "It's not Nicorette, is it?"

He chuckled. Then he said, "I'm actually a private detective."

"A dick? Why, yes, you are." He didn't laugh. Admittedly, it wasn't funny. "So...what's that mean?"

"It means someone hired me because they're being blackmailed. They think the blackmailer is you. Among other things, I'm trying to retrieve some lost property. That's why I was at the party."

"Someone thinks that I am capable of extortion? Me?" I was flabbergasted. "Me? Extort? I can't even cheat on a crossword puzzle. I'm the worst liar you've ever met. I stutter."

"I don't know about that, you seem pretty smooth."

"Are you high? I'm not smooth."

"You were last night. Very smooth, like a maître d'."

I grimaced. That was too close to home. "I was working. You know, this makes four of us in some kind of trouble. All of us were at the gallery last night."

"Four? You, the actor, my client and who?"

"Peter. My boss."

"Him? He's on my list as a person of interest." He exited the highway, turning onto a busy street filled with restaurants and markets.

"You're not a very good detective."

He drove the truck easily, chomping away on his gum. Poppy would have crapped herself if she knew I let anyone commandeer her darling, but I was a better passenger than I was a driver.

I peeked at him again, chewing my own gum and mulling over the facts. "The ring? Last night?"

"Part of the disguise."

"That's ridiculous."

"Yeah, well no one noticed me once at that damn party—I was just another guy. Except for you. No one. Not the waiters, the caterers, the artist, I was invisible to everyone except my client until you blocked my path and the door closed on my coat."

"Blocked your path?" I nearly snorted. "You stopped in the doorway, as if you knew me. I thought..." I thought my new blazer had mesmerized him. "Well, you don't want to know what I thought."

"I did know you. I was following you."

He put the blinker on and cut the wheel. We entered a sleepy tree-lined neighborhood. The houses were single family. The yards were tiny, but tidy. We were near Wagner College, the buildings lit on the hillside, and below us the Manhattan skyline was perfectly presented. It was stunning. Although it was still Staten Island. "This is nice."

"Yeah. Thanks. I took my grandparents' house after they went to Arizona a couple years back. My grandfather taught at the college." He parked in the short driveway of a handsome red brick Cape. There was a motorcycle under a tarp, otherwise it was neat as a pin. A tree grew in the front yard. The porch light was on.

"Wow. This is like the country."

He laughed. "Have you ever been to the country?"

"I went to Manhattanville."

"Well, this isn't the country, Romano. This is the burbs." Dan shut the truck off and opened the door. "C'mon. Have a beer before you go. We need to talk."

I shrugged. Like I had plans? I followed my new friend up the steps and into the house. "I guess I can have one."

"One, huh? You're a lightweight."

I smoothed a hand down my flat stomach. "Thank you."

He laughed again. "You're kinda funny."

"So they tell me."

The house was even nicer when we stepped inside, probably because anything larger than the guest bedroom at my grandmother's seemed palatial to me. The living room was to the right. There was a long sectional couch and a flat-screen TV and that was about all. I was relieved not to find pictures of dogs playing poker. Instead, there was a gorgeous Jasper Johns print hanging in a stark frame over the fireplace. Nice job, Detective Dan. Lots of controllers on the coffee table. I figured his grandparents had left some furnishings for him, and that he'd dovetailed the old things from his childhood with his own bachelor style. Bachelor? "So...uh...you live here alone?"

"Yeah. My office is here as well. You wouldn't believe how much of this job is spent on the computer."

He flung his leather jacket over the banister and so I flung my blazer there as well. I felt prissy. I should work on being less fussy.

We entered a well-stocked, homey kitchen through an arched doorway. Clean plates and glasses were piled on a smart wooden dish drain. A row of herbs grew on the windowsill in festive clay pots: spiky dill, thick-leafed basil and fragrant rosemary. I was impressed by the array of sharp, excellent knives stuck to a magnetic strip. The counter was butcher block, the walls a faded creamy yellow. A Viking refrigerator loomed in the corner. He even had a little braided throw rug in front of the back door. It was nice in a my-God-I'd-kill-for-my-own-place kind of way.

"Herbs? You cook."

"Yup. I want to open a restaurant some day." He nodded, handing me a Long Trail.

That had to be a joke, so I got right to the point. "Are you going to tell me who hired you?"

For a second, I thought he was going to stall. Instead, he bent. "Mallory Albright."

I choked and spat beer directly into his face.

"Jesus!" He jumped back, wiping his forehead with the sleeve of his shirt. "Man. What is your deal? You've got to be the most volatile—"

I held up a hand. "I'm sorry. I just can't believe that Mallory," *my savior*, "that she thinks...she actually thinks...she would..."

It was inconceivable. Mallory? Not Mallory. She was always so *nice*.

I kept sputtering like a child. "She...I...I...Mallory? She... I gotta go." I slammed the bottle down on the counter and made tracks for the front door, but Dan grabbed me by my sleeve with his wide, scarred hand.

He turned me around, saying, "God. You are such a feisty little motherfucker. I had no idea."

I clenched my fists, and my eyes bulged. "Say that again."

"*I had no idea.*" He had the balls to laugh. "Look. She and I both thought you seemed suspicious. You're in debt. You've got forty bucks in the bank. You're almost done paying off student loans. Peter gives you nothing. You live with your granny. And you're in and out of the galleries—you and the caterer. I think it's the blonde or one of her group, so that's where I'm looking next. But you look desperate enough on paper to commit a crime."

"Thank you." I burned with the shame of having my financial secrets laid bare. Mallory knew? I tore his hand from my shoulder. "Poppy isn't a crook."

"If you say so. Who do you think it is?"

"One of the waiters, or Brandon, or even Rachel. Jean Luc's in everyone's business. Shep remembers nipple rings."

He squinted at me, his face scrunching as he tried to follow. "Is that supposed to make sense?"

"Yes. If you were up to speed, you'd get it. What kind of detective did you say you were?"

"A good one."

I could hardly believe that. "What's Mallory missing?"

"That's strictly need-to-know," he said firmly. Dan didn't look like he could be moved on that. Actually, he looked like a smug bastard.

"I need to know." I couldn't believe Mallory would suspect me. That she hired someone to follow me. Disenchanted, I stood my full five foot ten, in these shoes, and said stiffly, "This changes everything. I could care less what happens now." She could take Justin Timberlake's goddamn head and stuff it right up her tight waspish—

"All right, Romano. Calm down. She's missing a painting. Someone took a painting from the gallery opening a couple weeks ago. The painting was...an interesting one. Actually, I think they'd call it something else—"

"A forgery?"

"No. It was just terrible." He tipped his bottle back and took a long pull.

"What?"

"Mallory put together a show—Flea Market Artistry: Found in the USA. You get what I'm saying? Salvation Army rejects. She collected all these pieces as a fundraiser, because money's tight everywhere and it was supposed to be a good time with low overhead. She sold tickets and was going to have it catered by your little girlfriend. She talked one of the Albright's most flush donors into loaning this, uh, postmodern unschooled acrylic. On canvas board. The backer? It was his mother-in-law's work."

I was barely listening. I had a bad feeling. "Postmodern unschooled acrylic? Really? That sounds..." Exactly like something I'd say. "What is it? The painting?"

"It's called Circus of Despair. I have a photo."

"You're kidding. I know that painting. I saw it in Steph's office, leaning on the bookshelf. She told me it was paint by numbers." Peter would have liked it though. He would have liked it a lot. He would have liked it enough to slip the damn thing inside his coat. Shit.

"Nope. So this backer reconsidered and asked for the painting back and...well there's no painting. He's hitting her where it hurts."

This didn't make any sense. "Why the hell would anyone think I took that?"

Dan shrugged. "Mallory suspects that you did it for Peter, to discredit the gallery—or that you're going to use it as leverage for a job."

I swallowed. "I wouldn't blackmail someone for a job. I'd

just ask for one." I bet I knew where that painting was. Well, at least where it was supposed to be. Peter and his proclivity for clown kleptomania. Jesus. A carousel and a harlequin, and my boss had a hard-on. That idiot. I swallowed. "How long have you been watching me?"

"I spent Wednesday doing your background checks—"

"Oh my God." Not that I had much of a background. Still, it was unsettling.

"Thursday and Friday."

I wracked my brain. Had I scratched myself? Picked my nose? Flirted ineptly? "Where were you?"

"On the train, in the Starbucks—you read a lot."

"How do you know Mallory?"

He stalled. "How don't I know Mallory? Her son represented me when I left the force. Got my settlement." He said this casually, glossing over some pretty major details. "Mallory and my mother are close. They went to school together."

I choked on my beer again. "Your mother went to *Smith*?"

Dan took one step and managed to fill the room. Had I insulted his mother with my tone? Maybe being alone in this stranger's house wasn't one of my better ideas. The guy was half a foot taller than me. No one had any idea where I was. I backed cowardly away. He smiled, his mouth slightly crooked, and that dimple appeared in his cheek. Mischief turned his eyes a deep brown, like the most bitterly dark chocolate. I held my ground, waiting. He reached a finger, touching my temple, and pain sliced me.

I jerked back and smacked my head against the wall. "Ow!"

"You've got an egg."

"That doesn't sound good."

His hand brushed the side of my face and then he gave a

self-deprecating shake of his head, like he was unwillingly amused. Great, now I was the clown. He dropped his hand and headed for the living room. "So, Caesar Romano. C'mon in and tell me all your secrets."

I trailed after him, my beer in my fist. "Only if you tell me yours."

# Chapter Five:
# Detective Dan

Sunday I went in to the gallery at ten. I left Poppy's truck in the alley. Captain and Joseph were nowhere to be found, which I took as a good sign. Unlocking the door, I poked the alarm code in by rote. Today was a major workday. I flipped the lights and went to turn the front door sign to OPEN. Back in the kitchen, I brewed a pot of Fog Lifter. Time to enjoy another exciting day at the Stuhlmann Gallery working my tail off for nothing.

My life was going down the toilet.

I went to check the messages. Midway through the congratulations and hang ups, it occurred to me that I never opened that stupid envelope last night. Dan had not only distracted me with a couple beers and a humiliating round of Gears of War, he was a terrible detective. He'd agreed to help me, and because I was broke, all I could afford was an incompetent, albeit attractive, investigator. He hadn't once asked about that envelope. Great.

I ran back to the van and searched the floor. The damn thing was lodged under the seat. My cell started chirping as I stepped back into the kitchen. It was one McNamara, Sheppard.

"Hel—"

"Where were you last night?"

"Oh. Sorry. I was with a..." I paused. What could I say? A friend? Hardly.

My silence seemed to say it all to Shep who fairly screeched, "You were getting laid while I'm having the single worst crisis of my life?"

Laid? I had spent the early part of the evening being grilled and the later part of the night interrogating anyone who answered the phone. I was incapable of concealing my intent so I had flat-out asked if they'd seen anyone upstairs. If they'd had sex with a guest. If they'd stolen something. They were all pretty pissed when they hung up. Worse, that bastard Peter had yet to call me back. He was hiding in the desert with the Treefucker guy, letting me handle his mess.

"Shep. I wasn't doing anything but having a beer and trying to save your damned neck. And why I'm explaining myself to you is a mystery. If you'd let me finish, I'd have told you that I was awake half the night leaving messages and talking to anyone I can think of who was at the party. No news. Then my battery died and I went to bed. What did you do?"

"I'm freaking out. Chad is breathing down my neck about that part. He's suspicious, and that dinner didn't help me any. I have to be the poster child of unblemished heterosexual living. Estelle asked me if you were my boy toy and told me to get rid of you. She thinks I should *pay* you to be quiet. And that asshole who sent the video emailed again. He asked me for more money."

Pay *me* to be quiet? Jesus, why hadn't I thought of that? Sighing, I dismissed every whine he had except the last one. "How does he want you to pay him? Secret drop at an undisclosed location? PO box?"

"PayPal."

"*Are you serious?*"

"As a fucking heart attack."

"Well that should be easy to track. I think I may have someone who can help us."

"You can't tell anyone, Ce. No one. Not about this and not about us. I'm not kidding."

"But you, of all of us, need to go to the police, Shep. You were violated."

"I'm fine." He wasn't fine. I could hear it. He was in denial, not exactly new territory for him, I know, but one of these days he was headed for a breakdown. "I can't go, man. I just can't."

"This person could hound you for years. You know that right?"

His voice grew unmistakably hard. "I'll handle it. Once I find out who it is."

"Fine. You hang in there. Go have brunch with your mother or something. Take the train to Connecticut and have some lox at the club. I'll speak with you later. I'll have this Dan guy check things out. I'm sure he has software for that kind of thing. Forward me your emails."

I went back to work preparing the sculptures for shipment. We'd only keep a few of the busts. Everything else would go to either its new owner or to other galleries. A few would return to Jean Luc's studio in Brooklyn. I still didn't know what to do about Justin Timberlake...except to wait for the blackmailer to contact me. And wait for Dan to come up with something.

I spent the morning hauling all the pieces into the South Salon and then I got the North Salon prepped for Peter. Installation was not in my job description. God forbid I so much as straighten a frame in this gallery once it was on the wall.

I took a break at eleven thirty and just as I sat down,

Rachel wiggled in. She was a tall, bubbly, sweet girl, and I immediately recollected the condom on the carpet upstairs. I still wouldn't pick that thing up. "Hey. What are you doing here?"

Rachel kissed my cheek, her lips a full, wide, cosmetically enhanced cupid's bow, painted a rich cherry red. I knew she'd left a big smear on my face. "I need to get the last check, and Brandon said he left the warming oven here. They loaded the truck on Friday night, and he asked me to come back over here and get it. I have an old boyfriend who says he can fix it. My brother lent me his car."

"What oven?" I went to my office to find Poppy's final payment.

"The warming oven. Are you deaf?"

No, I was confused. "You guys took it the other night. It's not here."

She looked even more confused. She asked in her chipper, squeaky morning voice, "Oh, maybe Poppy took it? You're sure?"

"I'm positive."

Rachel flitted off to the kitchen. Her ass wiggled obscenely in her skintight black jeans, on her feet, another pair of dangerously high, flashy heels. She wore a red halter top and great big red hoop earrings that brushed her shoulders. She was just so trashy and adorable. I gazed down at my gray flannel pants and my blue button-down. I was dull as dishwater beside her.

"Oh, is that coffee?" She swung through the door. I followed.

"Help yourself."

She gave me a considered once-over. She did it again as

she poured her coffee.

"What? Do I have something on my face?" I patted my cheek, feeling for crumbs or dirt.

"No. I just...I wanted to ask you...Caesar...if...you...you know...if...you...*know*. About me. If Poppy said anything."

"Know what? My God. Spit it out, woman."

"Ce. This is a secret. You can't tell anyone."

I was hearing that a lot lately. "Yeah. Sure."

Rachel took a sip from her cup, then added two sugars. Stirring, her wrist jerking sharply, she blurted, "So at the party the other night, someone left an envelope in my handbag."

The envelope. *Shit.* I'd stuck it in my pocket when Shep called. Why did I keep putting off opening it? Because it was going to be expensive. And because, really, this was Peter's problem. Resigned, I showed her my own wrinkled white mailer. "Like this one?"

Her eyes widened with recognition. "Oh! Yes. Exactly. Wait. Did you leave it for me?" she asked in bewilderment.

"No. Someone left this for me."

"Really? For you? What's it got in it? 'Cause mine was...like a bill. It was like a bill for nine hundred dollars. This was in it." She reached into her snappy red purse and fished out a folded piece of paper. She pressed it delicately into her cleavage. "You can't tell anyone. Promise. Only Poppy knows this, okay? No one knows."

"Sure, Rach. I promise."

She unfolded the paper. It was a photo of a young man, a teenager. He was cute. He seemed familiar. I took a good look at Rachel. "Is that your brother?"

"No. Caesar. Ding-dong. Look at the picture."

I checked it out. "Holy shit." My head snapped up on my

neck. She was so girlie and curvy. The big hair and tits...I knew better than this. "Oh. My. God."

"Yeah. I know. That's me." She winked and preened.

"Are you...? Did you...?" I crossed my legs. It was all I could do not to grab my crotch. I knew a few trannies, sure, but I hadn't ever met anyone who'd done the full deed. I spent most of my time in the gallery—I rarely stepped outside the art circle or the old neighborhood. I was rather sheltered for a queer New Yorker, come to think of it. It was all I could do not to glance at Rachel's groin. "When?"

"A couple years back. I'm a girl. I was always a girl. Look how tiny my bones are. I was a...you know. Like a mix." I immediately thought labradoodle and coughed. I needed to get a grip. She continued, "A hermaphrodite, not an actual boy. I'm a girl. My parents decided I was a boy. They were wrong."

"And Poppy knows this?" How could she not have said? Not even when we were drunk? I would have spilled that secret.

"Yeah. Of course."

I remembered the condom again. "Oh man. Does Peter know?"

"No. *No!* I'm au naturel everywhere else. These babies are real." She held up her breasts. "Well they were, but then I had them slightly enhanced." She waggled them proudly.

Slightly? They were double Ds, and they came to her neck. I groped the counter for support. "How would anyone find this picture? Or know the truth?"

"I don't know. I had it in my purse to show Poppy—and then I guess I didn't notice it was missing until now. I really would rather certain people not find out."

Yeah, like half the U.S. Navy on leave. I felt like sitting down. "I would think not."

"You can understand that some people might think differently about me." She gave me a small, embarrassed smile, and I knew she was terrified. "Some people wouldn't want...uh...that to get out, you know?"

I decided to tell her everything. The bust, Peter, Shep, Mallory, Justin Timberlake and the Circus of Despair...it all flew out of my mouth in great detail.

"Oh, Ce. We're all being harassed...for what? Peanuts."

"I wouldn't call it peanuts." We stared at the envelope. "I guess I should open it."

It wasn't sealed. The flap was simply tucked inside. I slid out a badly printed photo—someone's printer needed ink. It was Justin Timberlake, with one ear. The watch where his right nipple had been was gone. That was probably still on the sink upstairs.

"Oh! He still looks great." Rachel beamed. "That man is so talented. I just love him." I didn't know whether she was referring to JT or Jean Luc.

I flipped the picture over and on the back was a dollar amount. It read: Five thousand dollars. I choked.

"Holy shit. Good luck getting that kinda cash. Are you sure this is for you? Maybe it was for Jean or Peter."

"No. It was on the truck. Damn it. Why me?" I wasn't being a martyr. I honestly had no clue why I was getting hit up for that kind of cash and not someone else.

I schlepped into my office to think.


Dan sauntered in at one with his motorcycle boots and his black leather jacket. He had a paper sack in one hand and a tray holding two coffees from Starbucks in the other. He brought the scent of gum and sunshine with him.

"I thought you were following me."

"Not anymore. Remember?" He smiled at my tone.

"Hmph. Who *are* you following?"

"On this case? I'm weighing my options. I spent the morning on the computer checking your orange friend."

I snatched the bag out of his hand. Inside were two cheese-cherry Danishes, and my stomach did a backflip with joy. "Oh. These are just perfect. Do I have to share?"

"I figured you had a sweet tooth." He handed me a coffee.

"Why? Does it show?" I asked cheekily. His gaze swept down my body. He took his time, smirking over some smart-aleck comment, no doubt. I turned around and headed for the kitchen. I felt him watching me. "So tell me, master detective, why you didn't ask me about that envelope last night."

"Figure it out, Romano. C'mon. I know that you can."

I took my coffee from the tray and added two and a half sugars. "You...opened my mail."

He nodded. "Of course. It wasn't sealed. But I didn't know what the hell it meant until you started babbling."

He sipped from his cup. I tried not to make a face. He was drinking coffee *unsweetened*. "Did you tell Mallory it isn't me?"

"Well, she's convinced that either Peter Stuhlmann is trying to discredit her or Posh Nosh is blackmailing her." Not quite on the mark. Each time he lifted his cup, I got another look at his left hand. Stripes of white were neatly lined across the backs of his knuckles. Like he'd been lashed or whipped. He saw me staring but didn't offer any explanation. Instead, he pushed through the swinging door with his coffee and the treat. "Okay, Romano, show me around this taco stand. Let's see what we can come up with."

I gave him the nickel tour while I inhaled my Danish. I tried not to be a pig about it, but I probably had crumbs on my nose. Dan checked the men's room where I'd found Shep, he looked at the watch, he peeked in the trash. He didn't say much, just sipped his coffee.

I unlocked Peter's office.

"Why's there a condom on the floor?"

I got a bit defensive. "It's not in my job description to pick up Peter's leavings."

"All righty then. But are you sure it's Peter's? If it's Shep's, that's evidence, should he report it."

"I guess...it could be anyone's," I admitted. I grabbed the not-so-secret key, and we headed to the fifth floor.

Dan whistled, impressed by the hidden stairs. "No one knows about this?"

We stood at the window, admiring the view of the alley and the backside of the buildings. The milk truck sat in front of the dumpster, which was poor planning on my part. Those guys were going to use it as a urinal. "Just Peter and I and any number of people he's here to have sex with. I guess."

He squinted at the van. "How 'bout you?"

"Me? Sure, I've been up here a few times, yes." I was purposefully obtuse.

"So Peter has illicit affairs up on the fifth floor."

"No. Peter has both rare and not-yet-understood artifacts on the fifth floor. He prefers the sex to be in his office—and he likes inappropriately young women. I think he likes to show off his etchings."

Dan licked a crumb off his thumb. His tongue swiped across his skin, and I had to look away. "Ah. Hey, who's that?"

Captain and Joseph appeared from around the side of the van. "What the hell? They better not have peed on that truck again."

He laughed, his tone deep and unexpected in the narrow stairwell. "You shouldn't leave the truck there. It's too pretty for them not to piss on."

The two of them loped over to their pallet, a bottle a piece in hand. I swear to God, it looked like scotch.

"They're just bums. They sit down there all day drinking. They're harmless."

"No. They're witnesses."

"When they're sober."

We climbed up to the fifth floor and, yadda yadda, I showed him the clown room. I found myself uttering, "Now you can't tell anyone about this."

"I'll be discreet," he said solemnly.

So, I let Dan in on yet another sworn secret. (The first being not to out Shep—which had lasted for, oh, two seconds. The second being about five minutes ago when on our cozy tour I mentioned Rachel's delicate incision into womanhood.) Bracing myself, I opened the door. This situation with Peter was still shocking to me.

It didn't seem as traumatizing for the good detective, although he did snicker once or twice. Then understanding sobered him. "What did you say is missing?"

"I didn't. And Peter hasn't said. But...he has a *compulsion*, that from his own mouth. I'm sure he took the painting from Mallory. It was at the last show." My phone rang while Dan poked around. It was Poppy. "Hey."

"Ce, listen. I just got messages from six different wait-staff boys, and they tell me that you're harassing them. What the hell is going on?"

"Always a pleasure to hear from you too."

LB Gregg

Dan was opening and closing drawers in the highboy. He drew out a small tackle box, tilting his head curiously, like an overgrown beagle. He mouthed, "Who's that?"

I turned away. He was distracting in his black leather and faded denim. He was also unsurprised by this new development with Peter, and that ticked me off. "Poppy, has anyone taken anything from you over the last few days or weeks?"

She was silent. I could picture her big blue guileless eyes. Finally she asked, "Why?"

"Because there's a lot of that going on. I need to know if someone is harassing you." I secretly watched Dan, who pulled a red ball from the tackle box and stuck it on his nose. He turned and grinned goofily at me. I covered the phone. "Could you please? I'm trying to focus."

Bastard winked at me.

Poppy seemed hyper. "Mallory Albright keeps calling me. She's called me like ten times since yesterday. I think she's stalking me, I'm not kidding. I'm off this weekend and I'll call her tomorrow. You know, she still hasn't paid me for the last gig. I doubt she's phoning on the weekend to pay her bill. Did you send her your resume yet?"

"Slow down. Where are you?"

Dan set the tackle box on the bed and searched the rest of the dresser. From the bottom drawer, he extracted an absurd pair of red and yellow wingtips. They were hugely disproportionate to...everything. He set those on the bed.

Poppy grew hesitant. "I'm away. I'm...God...I'm with my folks." She was tiptoeing around something. "I'll tell you more when I get back, okay? I just want some time to myself to think. There's lots of work coming in and I need a break."

"Fine. No one is hassling you?"

102

"Not really. Although, I'm telling you, more than a few people haven't paid me. That's always a hassle. Just...could you lay off the waiters? I need someone to show up for the next gig."

I said peevishly, "Sure, whatever you want. I need to use the truck 'til you get back."

"Of course you can. Don't take a tone with me, Mr. Tone Taker. I love you, don't be a douche. And don't grind my clutch." She disconnected.

Dan was holding a fright wig. "You know, your boss is a clown."

"Yeah. And you don't even know him."

White greasepaint stained his hand. In the box lay a wide array of colorful pots and sticks, brushes and sponges. There was a jar of Noxzema. That explained Peter's odd cologne. It just kept getting worse. Dan stuck the shoes back in the drawer. "I wonder if it's a sexual thing."

Yes. Still getting worse. Peter having sex in clown shoes? Ugh. "Well. There's an image I didn't need. Thank you."

From downstairs the bell rang and we both froze. "Shit." I took off, flying through the apartment as the buzzer buzzed insistently. It rang and rang. Some idiot was holding the button.

I raced down the stairs two at a time, crashed through Peter's office, and took the corner around the desk at a sprint. The ball of my foot hit something slippery—the condom. I slid, my right leg buckled awkwardly behind my left, and once again I was flailing. I reached to grab the desk and latched onto the Rodin. That damn statue was a pain in the ass. It tipped, and we both hit the carpet with a hollow *doink*.

The statue split in half.

The buzzer buzzed, and I was sprawled on my belly on the carpet with a used rubber on my shoe. Dan ambled past me.

"You are such a spaz, Romano." He pointed at my shoe. "Don't touch that with your fingers."

Dan breezed down the stairs—his dark hair disappeared as he went to answer the door. I despised him at that moment. I hauled myself to my feet, scraped the condom off my shoe with a broken piece of Rodin, and decided that without question Peter was a tool.

Voices floated up the stairwell. I went to see who was below, but froze at Dan's words.

"Sure. Captain, you said? Yeah. You can use the bathroom. Second door on the right."

# Chapter Six:
# Sex, Lies and Apothecary Cabinets

"I really think that we need to look at your friend the cereal guy." Dan was using the wireless in my office while I finished prepping the Pappineau monstrosities. He dwarfed my spindly desk—which was actually a very nice Sheraton side table. Not a real desk at all. Just one more of Peter's beautifully collected pieces. It would be nice to have an actual desk. One that was broader, with sturdy drawers, and thick, masculine legs. I'd use a real leather blotter. That side table just screamed *queen*.

I put down the bubble wrap. "Shep's not a friend. Poppy is a friend. He is my former roommate."

Dan tipped back on my fragile, antique chair while I waited for it to crumble under his weight. He steepled his fingers, obviously thinking grand thoughts. "Sheppard McNamara. He's a famous straight guy who wants to play romantic leads. And you two were lovers, right? For years."

"Yes. Three years. Where are you going with this?"

"He's afraid of you. He must be terrified of his cousin. Men will do a lot of things to keep their secrets hidden. Lie. Cheat. Steal. I see it every day."

"Well, he didn't violate himself. I'm telling you. I saw the video."

He shrugged. "That may be true, but how do you know the video is recent?" He tapped away on the keyboard, and then whistled. "He's loaded. Someone must have died and left him a windfall. We should go visit him." I must have made a face because Dan added, "To have a jumping-off point."

"He didn't steal a painting. He was too drunk to walk. He's not involved."

"He's a lead. I need to speak with him. He must remember something."

"I am not going over there. He's out at his mother's anyway." Maybe. "Besides, I don't know where he lives. You'll have to look it up."

Dan put the chair down with a bang. He closed the computer and stood. The man flipping towered over my frail furnishings. He grabbed his jacket.

"Where are you going?"

"C'mon. We can say we were in the neighborhood or something and we wanted to talk."

"Can't you see that I'm working?"

"Caesar. Not a single customer has walked through the door since I got here. Just that bum who used the can. You can wrap the knickknacks tomorrow. Flip the fucking sign and let's go. We're not getting any closer to finding Mallory's painting or your...bust." He said that with a gleam in his eyes and a quick look at my pecs.

But he did have a point. "Why do you need me?"

"To get in the door."

What could I do? I capitulated and, as we turned the lock, I almost fell over Joseph who'd tucked himself into the back doorway. At his feet, a KFC bucket was full of chicken bones. He was greasy and as sour as pickled eggs.

"Hey." Dan nudged our resident vagrant with the toe of his boot. "You awake?"

Joseph curled more deeply into his dirty jacket. "A'yup."

"Did you go into this place yesterday? Through that door?"

Joseph nodded. I stared at the man, my jaw slack. "No way. You were unconscious. I saw you."

Dan ignored me. "For twenty bucks—and a free pass at not getting your ass kicked—who sent you in there and what did you do?"

Rheumy blue eyes barely focused. Joseph slurred, "I put that thing on the table and he give us some cash. Cap'n kept watch."

I felt like an idiot. "You guys made more money yesterday than I did."

The afternoon light slipped behind the buildings and everything lay in purple shadow. I was hardly surprised when Captain appeared from behind the van. I regarded him with a renewed sense of distrust. They were both crafty bastards, even if they were wasted on scotch. I was this close to asking him for my money back.

Captain stumbled over in grimy wet boots. He joined us on the stoop. He reeked of a desperate life on the streets—the foul concoction of garbage, urine, alcohol and deep fried chicken. "Yeah. He was the guy with the ball cap. He was sort of dark complected."

"That's not even a word," I snapped. "Was he dark skinned or was his complexion dark?"

"Is too. Look it up."

Dan tried to silence me with a quelling look. "Funny how?"

"He was white, but he was also odd. I dunno. We was sort of liquored up."

I knew where Dan was going with this, and he was wrong. "That's Brandon. He was burned when I saw him."

"Could be. We'll check him next. But it could also be your friend. His tan was pretty deep when I saw him."

I turned to Captain and Joseph. "Did someone pay you to tell us this crap?"

"Nope."

"They probably paid you to say that too." I'd had enough. Dan shelled out more cash for both the men while I stormed off toward the truck. I wondered if he should ask them for a receipt. Did Mallory cover his expenses? He should have kicked their asses. *I* should have kicked their asses, but I wasn't about to touch either of them.

There was another puddle on the tire. "You guys need to stop pissing on this truck. Do you hear me? Before I call the cops."

Dan grabbed my sleeve and practically threw me into the driver's seat. "Can it. We can hit the car wash. It's only pee. Relax and drive."

I waited for him to get in. "I bet they have typhoid. Or...syphilis."

"Nah. Probably just Hep C." He fumbled with his BlackBerry, thumb typing, then rattled off Shep's address. "Those guys aren't as harmless as they look."

"No kidding."

"You're just pissed that they got the better of you."

"I'm pissed that they took my lunch money yesterday."

We headed jerkily uptown to the tony address neither of us could afford in this lifetime, and I reflected on my prospects. I had hoped for a job with Mallory, working my way up...toward what? I wasn't a curator. I was an assistant. My interest in art had been fueled by a passion for freedom of expression...and a single-minded determination to stay out of the family business. I was blazing my own trails, and they had nothing to do with my heritage. Unfortunately, they were taking me nowhere. Where the hell was I going? Deeper into debt, that's where. I either needed that job with Mallory, or I needed to find a new direction. Those were my options.

"You want me to drive?" Dan asked again when I ground the gears and stalled at a light on Third.

"I'm fine. I can drive. You're making me tense."

"Your driving is making me tense, Romano." He adjusted his seat belt and snapped his gum.

By the time we finagled our way into Shep's building and up to the fifteenth floor, I was jiggling with nerves. Dan strode confidently down the hall. He probably did this all the time—wheedled himself into places he shouldn't. Peeping and lurking. But I was having second thoughts. Third thoughts. "I don't think that this is at all a good idea."

"What's the matter with you? We're here legitimately. We're stopping by to help him find out who his new boyfriend is."

"That's not funny. He's going to kill me for even telling you." Perspiring, I waited as Dan knocked. A half second ticked by, and I turned to leave. "He's not home. Let's go."

Dan knocked again, this time with more force.

I found the keys to the truck. "I'm telling you, he's in Connecticut visiting his mother."

Dan glanced at my hand for a beat longer than necessary. I could almost see an idea formulating in his big hairy head. Pity I couldn't read his mind fast enough, because he snatched those keys from my hand before I could hide them behind my back. "Hey. Do you think his cousin has a spare key? I bet she does."

"Give those back."

He quickly matched keys to locks, ignoring my protests. He easily blocked me from my wild grabbing.

I punched his shoulder hard. "What the hell are you doing? We can't go in there. That's against the law. You're a cop. You can't do this. I...I don't break the law." Protesting got me nowhere. I checked the hallway. It was quiet and empty. I could take him down with a surprise tackle. It worked on my brother and he was almost as tall.

"You do too. You pulled an illegal u-turn. You parked in a bus stop. You closed the shop when it should have been open. I bet you cheat on your taxes."

I stopped. "*I do not.*"

But he was already in the apartment. He grabbed my sleeve and hauled me in after him, then gently shut the door. The locks clicked. "Well, I knew that would shut you up."

"Oh man. This is so wrong."

"Quit being a crybaby. Look. Do you or do you not want to keep your job?" He stopped in what looked like a large foyer and whistled loudly. "Wow. This is a nice place."

My eyes bulged. It *was* nice. A *foyer*. It was vast—open and bright. What the apartment lacked in view it made up for in sheer square footage.

I forgot everything else. I huffed, and Dan gave me a stern look. "It's two apartments made into one. Don't get all excited."

"I don't know what you mean."

I had to check this out, illegal or not. I was in the door and now I was brimming with...an unflattering resentment. It looked like Pottery Barn had thrown up the contents of an entire catalogue in Shep's gargantuan home. Everything was picture-perfect and color-coordinated and made overseas.

"Track lighting," Dan scoffed. "That there is what we call a dead giveaway. No straight man lives like this. I don't care what you say."

"Did I say anything? He didn't live like this at Manhattanville."

The living room was bigger than my entire first apartment. I ran my hand the smooth length of a reproduction apothecary cabinet. Above that homogenized knockoff, a state-of-the-art flat-screen TV was centered with precision. A friendly grouping of leather club chairs sat in front of a white brick fireplace. On it, a wooden sailboat, three feet tall, sailed the mantle toward a humidor filled with cigars. You just knew they were Cuban.

I felt mean.

Dan disappeared into the kitchen. The sound of doors opening and closing followed him. He popped out of the doorway like a jack-in-the-box. "No Circus of Despair."

"Color me surprised."

He shook his head yet again. "Don't be a bitch, Caesar."

I swallowed. He was right. "Let's just hurry, okay? I'm not good at this kind of thing."

He proceeded to systematically search every nook and cranny in the thousands-of-square-feet apartment. I went to explore the rest of the space, curbing my bitterness. It was hard to do, as all I wanted was a humble apartment of my own. Anywhere. I'd take Staten Island, for crying out loud. And this? This plush bachelor pad looked ready for a spread in *Architectural Digest*—and it was utterly impersonal. There wasn't a single photo on the wall that hadn't been matted and framed in some sweatshop in China. On the dining-room table sat a gigantic glass bowl of wooden limes. Limes, for God's sake.

I needed to get a grip. I stomped inelegantly down a long hallway cheerfully lit with natural light, taking it all in, dollar

111

signs rolling in my head. Where had he gotten this kind of cash? Wheaties apparently paid Shep pretty damn well. The walls were papered in fucking linen.

"Hey. Take a look at this."

Dan was in the second bedroom, a guestroom as beautiful as the rest of the place. A four-poster king-sized bed took up most of the room.

"What?" I grouched.

The front door rattled and, horrified, I grabbed Dan by the jacket. "I knew this would happen."

I dragged him toward the closet, but it was overflowing with neatly hung clothing and stacks of shoeboxes. I gaped in shock. "Ferragamo?"

Dan nodded toward the armoire. I shook my head.

We both stared at the bed.

There was a lot of clearance, given the thing had stairs. I lifted the bed skirt. "Slide under."

The front door opened to the sound of Shep's charming, lackadaisical voice as we scurried under the bed like the fearful intruders we were. I flipped the bed skirt down. There was barely three inches of space to see. Dan lay flat to better watch the hall, although what we would do if we were discovered wasn't clear to me. I just closed my eyes and concentrated on not hyperventilating.

"Calm down, Romano."

I peeked and Dan wasn't paying attention to the crack of daylight. He watched me. I swear he was laughing. I nodded stiffly. I'd have to accept that I was a source of entertainment for the demented detective.

Shep's voice got weaker momentarily—perhaps he'd gone into the bathroom or the kitchen, and another voice, this one female, filled the apartment.

"That's Estelle. His agent," I whispered.

She was loud. "I don't care. You need to do as you're told or this thing is going to fall through and this is a huge opportunity. You signed a contract, Mac."

"I know. I don't think anyone knows."

"Everyone knows. You could have warned me last night. I had to listen to him rant for half an hour. That bastard will sue us both. Don't fuck this up."

They were in the living room. The sound of feet on the wood flooring came nearer. Unless Estelle wore fancy man shoes, that had to be Shep. He went into the room next to us. A door opened. He was changing maybe.

"I'll deal with it. Caesar isn't going to tell anyone. He hasn't yet. And his family doesn't care. No one else knows. I was circumspect. It was just a stupid thing I did in college. It was years ago. It didn't mean anything."

I nearly popped out from under the bed. Dan grabbed hold of my wrist. "Be still."

Shep went on, "He was pretty insistent. I slept with him a few times, that's it."

I opened my mouth, and Dan's hand slapped down to shut it. "Shh." I nodded and his hand slowly slid away, his fingertips trailing my chin. Was he petting me?

The click of Estelle's heels faded, as did Shep's plodding, well-clad feet.

She snapped, "Who knew back then, Mac?"

"No one. No one except my cousin, Poppy. That's it. And Ce's family. That's all."

"No one since then, right? I need you to think about your answer because I'd rather be prepared to handle some kind of

PR situation than get blindsided. A good offense is the best defense. I want full disclosure. You understand?"

"I..." Shep's voice wavered, and my breath froze as hope reared itself. Would he do it? Could he? And then that spineless dick lied again. "No one. I'm not...I'm not gay, Estelle."

Dan snorted quietly next to me. "She's an idiot if she buys that."

"As long as we're clear," Estelle said and then a door shut. Locks spun.

I lay under the bed, in the sweating darkness, royally pissed. Dan faced me, but his eyes were rolled up—he was listening while I was fuming and embarrassed.

"I think they're both gone."

I tried to scurry out from under the bed skirt. Dan grabbed my belt. "Wait. He may still be here."

I nodded and eased back onto the floor. Dan's eyes darkened, if that was possible. His frown line had reappeared. His voice turned serious. "How long were you two together?"

"Three years."

"Man. You sure know how to pick 'em. What a dickhead."

"It was just a stupid thing I did in college." My joke was undermined by the depth of Shep's betrayal. You'd think I'd have grown immune by now. At this point every one of my secrets had been laid bare to the good detective. There was nothing left to hide—which was actually kind of liberating.

We lay still, listening to the hall clock. I wanted to go home and forget this entire day. No. That was a lie. What I really wanted to do was take a hatchet to Shep's apartment and bust that mother up. Maybe Dan would turn a blind eye?

It was close under the bed. Naturally, there wasn't a speck of dust, only gleaming floor. It smelled of lemon and Dan's leather jacket. I hadn't noticed before, but his cologne was spicy—like cardamom. Sultry and tangy. His beard was filling in, a true five o'clock shadow that framed full and soft lips—the top one less plump than the bottom. A tiny scar marred the right side.

Dan stared intently back at me. He seemed as curiously interested in my mouth as I was his. Before I could catch myself, I licked my lips. His mouth lifted into a slow, hot, sexy smile. I bit my lip, waiting to see where we were going. Tension crackled between us.

He moved closer, taking up most of the space. It grew even warmer under the bed. "You know what I think? I think you're a smart guy and you dumped him for being a pussy. He's still pissed."

"Probably you're right."

Dan's mouth was very nice. Masculine and broad. Why hadn't I noticed that before? I had no idea what Dan's story was, if he was into guys or bi or yet another straight guy willing to fool around, but suddenly, I didn't care. I was pissed. Why that turned me on, I couldn't fathom. Dan didn't seem to be in any hurry to move away from me. Quite the contrary. He challenged me with his nearness.

I moved and his gaze went from my mouth to my eyes. Heat curled in my groin. Dan's eyes filled with interest, and something else. Amusement.

"Don't say a word," I grumbled.

"Who me?" The grinning bastard. "I won't say a thing."

I inched forward, scooting close enough to seal myself against him from groin to chest, letting our bodies align. Waiting to see what he'd do. His breath caressed my skin, and the moment drew out long. The clock ticked in the hall. His smug smile deepened, charming me despite how infuriatingly cocky he was. Strong thighs pressed into mine, and he waggled his brows like a fool. But he was hardening against my crotch and...that was a surprise. He found me more than amusing—he was attracted to me. Aroused by me. Or he was into the getting-caught vibe. Maybe a bit of both.

His dick nestled into mine, and his neck flushed a deep, telling red. With the space between us gone, in the sweltering darkness, I found a reason to lay my mouth on his, gently, finding those lips deliciously moist and minty. I licked them. His taste was sweet, maybe a hint of nicotine and coffee, but mostly he tasted of that gum he liked to share.

Dan laughed against my mouth. "You going to do something interesting, Romano? Or just nibble on me?" He thought he was so funny.

"If you'd shut up for half a second, I'll show you." I gripped him by the belt with one hand, and kissed him, my mouth sliding over his, my fingertips digging right into his pants. I tickled the head of his cock. Why not? I knew what I liked. I figured he liked it too, because he groaned in surprise. His lips parted, and his hips snuggled back. The big lug. I tongued him wantonly, feeling him give, his mouth opening wide to welcome me. A tingle ripped down my spine at this unexpected pleasure. He was delicious. Sliding my hips against his, all thought of Shep and Justin Timberlake and missing clowns disappeared as I did my very best to wipe that fucking grin off Detective Dan Green's face.

I suckled his tongue, rocking my whole body, working to make him harder. He had a nice, fat dick, long and broad, his bush wiry and wild. Sticky come pearled up. Yeah. He was right where I wanted him. I curved my fingers to stroke him in a firm grip that let him know I'd jerk him off and he'd never forget it, and he groaned again. Deeper this time.

And then that bastard flipped me over on my back with a fast move, trapping my hand in his pants and forcing the air from my lungs. "I see where you think this is going, Romano. You're used to leading guys around by their dicks, right? Like that pussy, McNamara. Guess again."

Holy shit. A blazing mix of shock and lust fried me as he rammed me into the floor, his mouth stealing the very air from my lungs. He kissed me like he was trying to pull my soul into his body, his tongue tasting, his hand cupping my chin, his hips spreading my legs and pinning me. Aggressively butch. Harsh and tasty. Jesus, it was thrilling and unexpected. My skin was on fire. I made small noises and let him take whatever the hell he wanted, my cock impossibly erect, my balls aching.

My fist was stuck in his pants, wrapped around that strong, ready cock, so I kept hold, jerking him off while humping myself into his crotch like a bitch in heat. His hand slid under my hips, and he tilted my ass off the floor with his wide palm, lifting me so he could fuck against me outright. Bumping and grinding our erections together. "When we get out of here I'm going to fuck your little ass so hard. You like that?"

Soft pleas were breaking from me. I was too far gone to be embarrassed. "Fuck. Oh fuck yeah. Shit."

"Yeah. You like that." His hand clenched my thigh, pressing my legs wide and that was about all it took. I fucked my cock into his, cotton friction so hot it nearly scalded me. He circled my lips with his tongue, his mouth dirty, and I let him work me. "Yeah. That's what I like. Come on, you little fucker."

*Oh my God.* Who was this guy? Embarrassed, I still shattered like some kind of good little boy for his big daddy. I came so hard and freakishly fast I was squealing. I couldn't stop. His dick squirted into my fist as I spewed inside my own pants. Warm and wet. I wanted to taste him. Instead I closed my eyes and just gave myself to him. It was exhilarating and terrible and exhausting.

He eased his mouth, dragging each kiss out gently. I hung on, squeezing the last of the come from his dick, and he collapsed on top of me. We were slumped in a pile, absolutely zonked from that orgasm. I hadn't come with anyone else in a long time. I hadn't come like that ever.

"That was great, Romano. I knew it would be."

What could I say? We were strangers. "Mm."

It was Dan's turn to nibble. He lazily kissed my shoulder. "You wanna scoot out of here and get some work done, or do you want to go at it again?"


"It's no big deal, Caesar."

We crawled out from under the bed, careful not to smear body fluids on the furniture. "What if he'd still been in the apartment? That was totally unfair. You took me by surprise. I don't even know you. I don't usually have sex with strangers." Excuses spilled from my mouth in a torrent. My pants were damp. What the hell had I done?

"You started it, not me."

That was true. I searched for something to wipe my hand on. "Doesn't he own tissues?"

Dan handed me the box. "You're riled up, Caesar. You're supposed to be relaxed now."

"We needed to get out of here. It's only a matter of time before Shep comes back." I checked my watch. Only twenty minutes had ticked by since we snuck in the door. I'd never come that fast in my entire life. I flushed and snuck a glance at Dan. Understandably, this little scenario only made him more arrogant.

"You should be kissing my feet right now. You needed that."

I flipped him off. "You were pretty quick on the draw there yourself, Detective. Please. Let's just... Why don't you show me what you found so we can leave?"

He picked up a small book from the bedside table and flipped through it. It was a discreet, bound photo album. I guess Shep wouldn't want to offend anyone's design sensibilities by having a personal touch in his own damn house. I squashed my misplaced anger like an unwanted insect. Dan found the photo he was searching for and handed the book to me, saying, "I didn't realize they were all this cozy."

I stared at a four-by-six color glossy of Shep, his parents, Poppy, her parents, and what looked like the Schumachers— the blue-eyed zealot and his horse-faced bride. They sat together in a restaurant with none other than the artist himself—Jean Luc Pappineau. He wore a silly-looking pirate hat. "That's the country club. I've been there."

"You know the blond guy? He was at your dad's place."

"Chad Schumacher. The producer." It never crossed my mind that Poppy knew the man as well. She had a painful, slim smile on her face and a smoldering cigarette in her hand. I thought she'd quit. "He's a homophobe."

"He's Mallory's backer."

"What?" I stepped back. Dan nodded grimly.

"He's a patron. Mallory tolerates him. That's it." I absorbed that information. Dan opened a drawer in the nightstand and pulled out a flashlight. He stared at it and put it back. "You sure Shep went to the gallery to see you? Maybe he was going to see Jean Pappineau. Is he gay?"

"He's whatever the mood strikes. Divorced three times. I think he tried to get Peter to show him those etchings once or twice, but Peter didn't bite. Jean's a bit of a whore. He's an artist."

I set the photo album down. Shep at the gallery to see Jean? Now there was a thought. Because Jean Luc would have no problem fulfilling Shep's darker fantasies.

"Of course, he could be with your little blondie."

"Poppy would have said." Who was I trying to convince? She'd kept a few secrets lately.

Dan lifted his brow at me. "Well, Jean's there as someone's guest. Maybe he knows the parents, but I bet it's Poppy."

"She does like older men. The over-forty crowd."

"Watch it, Romano. That's not old."

I'd struck a nerve. "If you say so."

The hall clock bonged and I reared back like I'd been shot, clutching my chest. "We need to get out of here. It's six."

That fool unzipped his fly and went into the master bathroom.

"What are you doing?"

"I need to clean up. If you want to spend the evening in sticky underwear, that's your call. I don't want to chafe. C'mon, snap to. We need to hurry."

Was he fucking kidding me? "We need to get out of here. I think I'm having a panic attack."

"What else is new, Romano? Shake a leg."

It took me exactly five seconds to mop up, but I took another precious few moments to rip through Shep's bathroom, yanking open drawers and... I know. Why? It wasn't like JT was in the bathroom. But I was curious. All I uncovered was a drawer full of toys that I didn't know how to use. He was into some freaky stuff. I tried to picture Jean Luc stuffing a ball gag in Shep's mouth and, quite frankly, it wasn't that much of a stretch.

I shut the drawer on Shep's dirty secrets. It was like the more he'd denied himself, the more kinky he'd become.

I washed my hands and then I was at the front door, my eye plastered to the peephole. Dan was dragging his feet, all but whistling once again. Postcoital he was cocky. I was going to kill him. "Could you please hurry the fuck up?"

The hall was clear.

We slipped out and locked the door. We almost made it to the elevator too, but the light turned white and the doors slid open with a cheerful *bing bong.* As you would expect, Shep glanced up from his feet. His eyes widened with recognition. I felt the blood drain from my face.

"Caesar? What are you doing here?" he asked in confusion. He held a net grocery sack from D'Agostino's and a bottle of Pinot noir tucked under his arm. He blinked at Dan, struggling to place him. "Dan, right?"

"I...I...I..."

With a hand to my back, Dan shoved me into the elevator. He calmly stepped in beside Shep and offered his hand. Hopefully he'd washed it. "We were just dropping by, but obviously we missed each other."

"What a happy coincidence," I choked.

"I didn't think you knew where I lived. Do you want to come in? I bought some snacks." He lifted the grocery bag.

The elevator door slid shut with another *bing bong.* Dan poked the button for the lobby and lied with aplomb, "We're late for a movie, but we were in the neighborhood. I was telling Caesar I thought you should load some software on your computer; it'll help us figure out who sent the video. We can track the email. It's pretty standard for this kind of thing. You should think about it."

Shep turned an interesting shade of salmon. "You know about that?"

Dan shared his special smile with Shep. "Of course."

Actually, that was probably the best idea he'd had all day. I had to give the man credit. He was staying focused on his work (not counting those twenty seconds under the mattress). The man was deceptively laid-back, but I knew he was sharper than he let on.

Shep, who was not, turned to me in disbelief.

I held a hand up. "Hey, I mentioned this to you, Shep."

For the first time ever, I saw Easy Mac get angry. His hue electrified into raging sherbet orange and his knuckles whitened. "I told you not to say anything. You promised. What the fuck, man? What's the deal? This is my life."

*His* life? "Oh, knock it off and stop being a drama queen."

Dan stepped between us. "I'm not sure what you think is happening here. I'm trying to locate stolen property, as is Caesar. We both believe the sender of your video is connected to whomever is blackmailing my client and my new pal, here." He jerked his thumb over his shoulder, pointing to me. His pal. "We're not going to put your career in jeopardy."

"You'd better not. I'll sue you both for libel."

"Slander," I corrected him. "You moron." They both looked at me like I was crazy, but what could anyone take from me? My bus pass?

Dan handed Shep a card. "Call me. We should talk. If you need help, I can track this person down."

The elevator ponged, announcing our speedy arrival to the

lobby.

I tried to exit, but Shep grabbed my shoulder, stopping me in the threshold. His grip wasn't friendly. "Caesar. I need you to promise that you'll keep your mouth shut. Please."

I knocked his hand away. "Well, I have needs of my own, Sheppard. Since no one wants to involve the police, we either help each other or I'm going to tell each and every one of you to go fuck yourselves. I'll go to the police myself, because I have nothing to lose. If I find out you're lying, I swear to fucking God, I'm going to come back here and kick your ass." My hands were waving around beyond my control. I clenched my fists, stuffed them into my pockets and exited.

The sound of Dan smacking Shep on the back followed me. "Nice place you got here."

I caught Shep's shocked expression as the door sounded again and promptly closed.

"You've got a wet spot on the front of your pants," Dan said happily.

"I know. So do you. I think I need to talk to Poppy."

"That blonde and her people are looking more and more interesting." He checked his watch. "I need to get back to the office."

The street lamps sparkled up and down 57th Street. The air had turned cold. I finally admitted to Dan, "I'm confused. I just can't see Shep with Jean Luc. Or Jean Luc with Poppy."

"I could see either of those men with a donkey. Are you saying the McNamaras are discerning when it comes to men?"

He made yet another good point. "That was a good idea. The email. Because...Shep is scared."

He nodded.

"I think we need to look at Brandon. He's orange, he was

there. He could have fucked Shep—but he's straight. I mean, no way would he ever."

"You're sure."

"Absolutely. So between Justin, Rachel, Peter, Mallory and Shep, there's a common thread, and it's me and Posh Nosh. I know that Poppy would never threaten me. Or Shep. Or Rachel. Mallory. Peter. It doesn't add up. She has no motive. Nothing to gain." I unlocked the doors to the van. Dan climbed in and we sat there in silence.

"Someone has a motive, we just don't know what it is. I need to see that video. I need to get back home and work."

# Chapter Seven:
# Staten Island Fairy

"Turn here."

"I remember. I drove back. I've got it."

"You're a terrible driver. I don't mind driving. We can pull into that 7-Eleven."

"I'm fine," I said for the tenth time. I took the bridge to Staten Island at a safe, comfortable, forty-five miles per hour. I borrowed ten bucks from Dan to pay the toll. He sat in the passenger seat, snapping his gum and offering driving tips, as the miles thumped under the tires. I think he was trying to ease me, because there was no question he wanted to continue what we'd started earlier.

By the time we arrived, my stomach was moaning. I hadn't eaten since that Danish.

"Can you cook?" Dan asked, throwing his jacket on the banister again. "I need to take care of a few things. Why don't you...make some eggs or something?"

Could I cook? I was a Romano. "A little."

I used Dan's fancy kitchen while he worked. I focused on making spinach frittatas, a simple recipe that included stuff he had in the fridge. He had fresh spinach and an All-Clad omelet pan. He was serious.

He went into the office, which turned out to be the other half of the downstairs. I whipped the eggs, crafting a tasty supper in that perfect pan.

Dan's muttering carried from the other room. I used the bathroom and stared at myself in the mirror, wondering what the hell I was getting myself into.

The timer dinged. I made good rye toast, piled everything onto plates and carried the lot, waiter style (because I'd been trained by the best), to his desk. A desk that wasn't at all spindly, in case you were wondering.

He looked up from the computer. "Shep is loaded. I don't understand why he doesn't pay you to be quiet."

"Because he knows I wouldn't take it. Move on." I took a seat in what had to be the client chair. The eggs were too hot, so I tackled my toast. It was slathered in whipped butter. I licked crumbs from my fingers, Dan's steamy gaze following me.

He cleared his throat. "Jean Luc. He's in debt to his eyebrows. He poured everything into these new works. I think you may have more assets than he does." He shoveled eggs into his mouth, scrolling through Jean's work. The images flew past. "Hey. This is good."

"Why are you surprised? I'm a Romano. My family cooks, *Detective.*"

A photo from the other night appeared, and Dan clicked to enlarge it. I swallowed a mouthful of bread. How wonderful that the art world had a current photo of Jean standing on the bar. Shep stood smiling at Jean's ass in the background. He was ripped and sloshed. The bust of Derek Jeter was settled between Jean's knees, facing the wrong way. That was a bit much.

"He pays a lot of alimony, from what I understand."

Dan clicked again. "Did you know Peter went to clown

college?"

I choked on my dinner. "What? No. He went to Boston College. I realize some people think that they're the same thing—"

"He went after a year at clown college."

"Oh my God. Does Mallory know that? That would completely discredit him. I mean...you know...not that there's anything wrong with being in the circus—uh." Hopefully no one in Dan's family worked for the Cole Brothers, or Coney Island. "Well, the art world is very discriminating. How in the world did you find that out?"

Dan shook his head at me. "Don't you Google? My God, Caesar, you're twelve years younger than I am and it's like—"

"I know how to use the computer. Who do you think maintains the gallery website, the brochures, the email...I handle the restaurant, the printers, I built my Uncle Tino's entire site. I just never thought to Google my boss. It's creepy."

He grinned unrepentantly. "Well, that's my job. Professional creeper. I even Twitter. Let's Google you."

I sat there mulling over the Twitter comment. He typed my name in and a pathetic fifteen items appeared. All but one mentioned the gallery. I didn't even have a life online. "So I went to parochial school. That's about it."

"Your family is suspiciously absent from the internet, did you know that? Other than the basic business information and foodie reviews. That's pretty interesting."

"I don't know what you mean."

Dan tipped back in his chair, his arms clasped behind his neck. He measured me. "Why did you go to work for Peter?"

"It was a good job for me at the time. I like organization. I'm good at managing unmanageable people. I guess I thought it would be exciting, and sometimes it is. Like the other night. It's fun. But it's not particularly rewarding. Although the artists are refreshing."

"They are."

I chewed, keeping my eye on Dan, who kept his eye on me. What was he thinking? "Hey. What about Brandon?"

"Brandon's been around the block. He's all over the net, but his nose is clean. He's from Boston, originally. Beacon Hill."

"What's that? Old money?" That well had long dried up.

Dan stood. From my seated position, he was huge. "So." He smiled. "Let's pick this up later."

"Oh. Oh yeah. Sure." I wiped my mouth and scrambled to get moving, grabbing my plate and my iced tea. Nothing worse than overstaying your welcome. I was unreasonably disappointed, but I should have realized he had things to do. "I'll just...clear this...and then—"

Dan's hand landed on my biceps, halting me in my tracks. His voice was low. "That's not what I meant." His fingers closed and he dragged me backward. I juggled my dish, but my plate slid and my fork bounced with a tiny thump on the carpet. "Leave it." He took my plate and set it on the desk, and then his rough hand slid down to mine. His touch burned. Was that even normal?

"Uhm. All right," I said weakly.

He led me from the room and down the shadowed hall. We took the stairs. I watched his beautiful ass move inside his jeans as his boots hit the treads, and still he held my hand, dragging me to his lair.

I had enough time to catch three open doorways before he ushered me into a smallish bedroom. The hall light revealed walls a deep rich blue. The furnishings were walnut. It was striking and masculine. A lot like the man who was tugging me firmly toward the bed. I sputtered, "So I...uh...take it you don't want to play video games?"

He whipped his shirt over his head and I shut the fuck up. The sight of a half-dressed Dan Green and words failed me. His chest was covered in a V of beautiful dark hair that dipped down into a low-slung waistband. He defined definition. I mean, the man was ripped and scarred and mouthwatering. Narrow bands of light streaked his skin—street light coming through the blinds. Mr. Noir Detective on the make. I licked at my dry lips, and he slid his arm around me, drawing me near. "I told you what I was going to do to you."

I swallowed. "Uhm. I thought that was, you know, sex talk. Because, I'm...not usually that...kind of boy. Actually." I was more a giver than a receiver.

Dan cradled my hips into his very prominent erection. He said huskily, "I know exactly what kind of boy you are, Romano."

He took my rough chin in his hand and settled his mouth on mine, his kiss scorching, dominating. I kissed him back, tangling my fingers in his chest hair. I gripped him almost painfully, and he growled low, nipping my lip. Our teeth scraped, and his hands cupped my ass, lifting me against his crotch. Without a thought, I climbed his body and eagerly wrapped my legs around his hips.

"Yeah. That's what I'm talking 'bout."

"Oh shut up."

He tipped back, and this time around we were on top of the mattress, the comforter a gorgeous brown like his eyes. I straddled Dan's hips, feeling him up, down, gripping and stroking and finally smoothing the puckered skin on his arms and shoulder. They were burns. He'd been burned.

Dan buried his hands inside the ass of my pants, sliding around to hold me with the flat of his palms. "Where'd you lose your underwear, Caesar?"

His whiskers were sharp. My tongue rasped along his jaw. "I think I lost them downstairs."

He smiled and squeezed—broad fingers circled in to brush against my balls, then the sensitive spot where my ass curved deep. A fingertip sought out that tight, shy, dark place. I tensed. I couldn't help it.

"Let's take this off you too. Lift up." He purred and took my shirt off me, undressing me like a virgin. Which, he was about to find out, I nearly was. All kidding aside, I'd fucked a few guys, but it wasn't something I much liked in return. I found that having a guy stuff his boner up my ass hurt like hell.

"Dan. I..."

He rolled with me, putting me on my back, murmuring, "Shhh...let's just take these off of you." Kissing, coaxing, seducing me. Leading. I toed off my shoes and they tumbled to the floor. Dan's sweet mouth moved down to lick my armpit, my nipples, my navel—he drew my middle finger into his mouth and pleasure flooded my crotch. I watched him suck on my skin. He was beautiful. I stroked his hair, his shoulders, his neck, anywhere I could reach. I just wanted to feel him, puckered, smooth, firm, wiry-haired, gliding under my hands. It had been so long—too long—since I'd done this. Since I'd felt this.

He tugged my zipper down like he was unveiling a gift, spreading my pants open. "Yeah. There it is. You have a nice fat dick. I would have never guessed it."

"I'm Italian," I said inanely.

"Lift up." He peeled my clothing away. Moist, petal-soft heat closed on my cock. Dan's mouth slid leisurely from the tip of my dick to the root and I free-fell into a pit of lust so deep my hands fluttered wildly and then clenched into fists. My eyes rolled back in my head. He used the flat of his tongue, the roof of his mouth, man, could he suck cock. He wouldn't take it all the way, though, not after that first time. I grabbed his neck to stuff myself deeper, but he snatched my wrist, pinning it to the bed. Oooh-kay. I'd just, wait here, while he...oh...God...worked my stiff flesh down the succulent depth of his throat.

I made a noise. "Mmrph."

His lips came popping off the end of my prick. He nipped my inner thigh, licking a trail over my tight balls, nuzzling my hair, and then his mouth slid lower to my ass. He tucked both my wrists under my hips, holding them with one hand, raising my entire bottom so he could feast on my hole. Trapped and exposed, I squeezed shut my eyes, tensing, but his tongue soothed me, slipping and relaxing, easing me, preparing me, loosening... Oh shit. I was going to come.

"I'm...I...I..."

Dan's mouth closed on my budded opening, now so ready for something. He let go of my wrist, pushing my knee high. "Hold your knee."

I did and he fucking slurped on me, and then his grip closed on my cock. He was rimming me, jerking me. I'd not ever...because Shep wasn't...no one had...it was...like nothing I'd ever experienced. Airborne. Wild. Tearing, gripping want ripped through me. I needed him to finish me right now. Right this fucking second. My toes curled. My hands dampened. My nuts shriveled like raisins. Dan's hot hand stroked me, his tongue lapped...and he moved away.

Balanced on the precipice, I dropped my knee and clutched at him. "No. *No*...n...oh...I'm going to come."

"Yeah. You are." He spread my knees and slid a finger deep

into that tight channel. He hit my prostate. It was perfect; perfectly timed. Sparks sizzled along my spine. His mouth closed on the head of my dick, and I came round that crazy bend gasping and desperate and stuffing my cock, pumping it right inside his sucking, lovely mouth. He swallowed, the sound soft in the room, and a second finger spread my chute. Goddamn, he was caressing the inside of my body, his fingers spearing, and somehow, he coaxed another wave of orgasm.

My heart drummed madly against my ribs. "Oh. Don't stop. Oh God. Don't stop."

He didn't. He drew that climax out until I was wrung dry and weak.

I felt him smile as he let go. I opened my eyes and found Dan anything but smug. In the harsh streetlight slicing through the blinds, he looked fierce. He wiped his chin with the heel of one hand, and drew his fingers from my body. He sat back and dropped a boot on the carpet, his eyes never leaving mine.

Sprawled. Willing. That's how I felt. Mind blown and royally fucked. I slumped into the cozy bedding. Dan didn't give me a moment to collect my feeble thoughts. His voice cracked through the bedroom, authoritative and thick with need. "Turn over." The other boot dropped.

I rolled over lazily, not really one to appreciate authority figures, and waited. His belt buckle clacked, jeans slid in the quiet room, and I got a good look at him. Strong, hairy, thickly roped with muscle. The scars were limited to his arms and shoulders, a few lines on his ribs.

He prowled up my body, that handsome face dead set on his goal. Which would be me. The end goal, as it were.

Lips touched my skin, starting at the back of my knees. Dan's mouth feathered hotly along my legs, over my backside and onto my lower back. His hands were busy, massaging my spine, stroking to my shoulders and neck. He licked a path to my nape. His cock trailed wet along the crack of my ass. I wasn't too spent to stop myself from flinching.

"Open your legs, Caesar."

I did. Dan nipped my neck.

"Up. Get up, on your knees." He knelt over my back, giving me room to lift my hips in the air for him. "Don't get all tense. I'm not going to hurt you."

Yes he was. I knew it down deep, but I nodded, my forehead scrubbing into the pillow, the soothing scent of Downy filling my head. Dan fumbled in the drawer of the small table by his bed. Lube. Condom. Hopefully nothing else. I...couldn't imagine we'd need anything else.

Broad thighs widened my legs, opening me. I should be more responsive or encouraging, but I was too busy trying to relax. Too busy trying not to be embarrassed.

"I'm going to slide right in, you're ready. You're perfect." His fingers dipped inside me, demonstrating his point. He smeared me slick with lube, and I moaned when he grazed that spot. Oh God. He murmured, "Yeah. You'll see. You're going to love this. You were made to be fucked, baby."

That dirty mouth sucked my neck, love-biting me, and lust bit me again. I wriggled, pushing back into him. He was deftly finger-fucking me with three spread fingers; they stroked and pet me, and I was perking up. It tingled and burned, but not painfully.

"Yeah, that's it, rock back on my fingers. You're so ready." I swear he was smiling against my neck.

Dan shifted, his fingers disappeared from my crack, and then fat, hot, latex...he breached that ring. I tensed, but there was no pain as he slid in, slid all...the way...in. Exactly like he said. He bit me again and I hissed. Full, stretched, uncomfortable—I was also arching into him impatiently. He gripped my hips, settled his knees—I guess just the way he liked it—and he worked my hips on his cock. My breath hitched with each and every stroke as he fucked against my prostate. I'd never felt anything like it before. It was good. It was so goddamn good. My cock grew, semi-erect, bobbing between my thighs. I had to touch it.

"That's it, baby, grab your dick. Fuck yourself." He banged into my backend, fingers digging into my hips, and, yeah, I jerked myself off, feeling slutty and hot and wide open for his cock. The bedframe hit the wall as he slammed inside me. I licked salted sweat from my lip, moving fast and furiously, and I was flying along with Dan, swearing, sweating, grunting on every exhale. Our bodies slapped together in that effort to merge. That most perfect union. It was old, it was new, it was frighteningly real. I lost my grip on the present, and then Dan went deep. He exploded inside me. His breath whistled through his teeth, and as he came, his cock lurched, spewing, trapped in his condom. "Come on, come on."

I came weakly into my own hand, just like old times. Not the shattering revelation of earlier, but a slow, tripping release, a ripple that was as much about relief as it was about sex.

Dan's hands caressed my back. We were drenched in sweat and sticky with come. He didn't slide out of me, didn't break his hold, didn't act in any way like I expected. He was in no rush to disengage from me. No. He was ever surprising. He turned, tucked me—sheltered me into his body, spooned me, held me, and his soft words fell against my cheek before his mouth found mine. "Thank you."

# Chapter Eight:
# The Albright

Monday morning I crawled from my tiny bedroom and stumbled to Nana's sunny kitchen, a little sore, a little bleary, a little hungry, and feeling pretty damn good. Adam Lambert couldn't have sung it any better. It was a new day.

Clearly, I needed to have sex more than twice a year.

"Good morning." Nana was awake, in her slippers and her good blue housedress. She had all her bracelets on, her face done, but her hair was still rolled in curlers the size of coke cans. I think she said they added volume. She stared with ill-concealed interest at my throat. "What's that on your neck?"

My hand crept to my throat of its own accord. I clutched my robe in my other fist. "I—"

She held up her hand, and jewelry cascaded down her arm in a clatter. "I don't want to know."

"That's wise." I sat down with the milk and Special K, my pleasant worldview intact. I concentrated on dumping sugar onto my breakfast. Bella twined around my ankles.

Bracelets clacked a warning. "Unless it has to do with that actor. Because, Caesar—"

"Nope." I stuffed a spoonful of cereal in my mouth.

Nana puttered. She was going to be late for her Monday morning senior's trip to the...somewhere. A museum? Maybe they were going shopping. Unlike my own empty dance card, she had so many social obligations it was hard to keep track.

In no hurry, she carried two cups of coffee to the table. Joining me, she took the sugar. She tried for subdued. "So. Tell me what's new in your life."

I sighed and set my spoon on the table. "Nan. I went out. I came home. I'm going out again. I'll come back home again." I mimed this process for her with flapping hands.

"That's fine. You're a grown man. I understand completely." She sipped her coffee, her brow furrowing. "Because I want you to know that whatever you decide to do, it's none of my business."

It took a lot of effort not to roll my eyes. I picked my spoon up and resumed eating my breakfast cereal. I added another spoonful of sugar. "Thank you."

I had a brief flash of Dan uttering those words to me last night. Heat burned my cheeks.

"And if you wanted to bring a new friend here, I wouldn't stop you."

A splash of milk covered the back of my hand. I'd lost hold of my spoon again. "Nana. I love you, but I'm not bringing anyone *here*."

She sniffed. Fortunately, I was saved by the ring of my cell phone.

It was Poppy. She'd taken long enough to return my calls. My texts. Maybe I should have Twittered.

"Ce?"

"Yeah. Where are you? I really need to talk to you."

"I'm...I'm having some trouble." Her voice tightened.

That wasn't right. Poppy didn't do weak. She didn't cry. Poppy swore, she broke things, she made people crawl. She didn't cry. I pushed my breakfast away, concern for Poppy overriding everything.

Nana watched me, keen to horn in. I shook my head, waving her away. "Please, Nan? Just give me a minute."

"Fine. I need to go tease my hair." She grabbed her coffee and left to find her Aqua Net.

"Hey. What's up? What the heck is going on, Poppy?"

"I think, I think...I may need to ask you for a favor. A really big favor."

I exploded. "Will you stop being cryptic and tell me what the problem is? Is that so difficult? You have no idea what's going on here. Shep's being blackmailed, Rachel's a man, Justin Timberlake is missing, I got laid last night two—no, three times, Peter's a goddamn clown, and today I'm supposed to throw myself on the mercy of Mallory Albright, who incidentally thinks I'm a circus-art thief, and beg that bitch for a job. I can't handle this crap. This is supposed to be a brand-new day." From the other room I heard Nana cough. I lowered my voice. "For fu-reak's sake, Poppy dearest, if you have something to say, say it. Because Detective Dan thinks you're somehow involved in this mess. Talk to me."

Phew. I was glad to get all that off my chest.

"If you'd shut your mouth for a damn second, Caesar Anthony Romano, I'd say something. Jesus. Get a fucking grip. First, who's Detective Dan? You mean Shep?"

I was all but whispering. "No. Could you please get up to speed? Detective Dan is this dick who's investigating a stolen painting."

She huffed at me. "All right. I'm on my way into the city. I have no idea what you're talking about...but I'm gone thirty-six hours and you got laid? You?"

Now that there was the Poppy I knew.

"That's what you got out of my rant?"

"Who? If you say Shep, I swear to God—"

"No. Stop asking me that. I...had an indiscretion. Multiple times. What the hell with Rachel, though? I cannot believe you didn't tell me that."

"I couldn't. There's too much going on. But...you need to know something, okay? Don't freak out on me. Promise me."

"What?"

She burst into tears. "I think I'm broke."

Broke? "That's impossible. You're busy all the time. You're growing."

"I know. I thought so too, but all these people aren't paying me—"

"I'm sorry. Was it my thing the other night?"

"No. And you did pay me, I just did that at cost. No. Mallory Albright owes me a lot of money. I'm supposed to do this gig tonight, it's a big schmooze, and I'm short. Plus...there's cash missing. I made payroll, but barely."

"I'll call Pop. I'll call Uncle Vito. They'll lend you some—"

"I asked my parents. That's where I went. I was in Connecticut."

"Holy shit." Connecticut? This was serious. "If someone's stealing from you, we need my family. We'll figure it out. Did you see your accountant?"

She hiccupped. "Yeah."

"Well. You need a new accountant. We'll call Joey. He'll know someone. He's got all those friends at Columbia."

Her voice got small. "Okay. I'm so embarrassed. I'm

heading in right now. I'm on the train."

"Fine. I'm going to Mallory's for that job. You know, her assistant, that Stephanie chick, she didn't say anything about this—that Mallory is tight on cash, or forgetful. That's weird."

"Please don't tell anyone. Trust me, it's not just the Albright thing. I'll...meet with the accountant."

"What you need is muscle to go get your money back."

"I know. I...thought I had someone, but it's just a big clusterfuck."

My phone beeped. "Hold on." It was Dan. "Hey."

"Hey. How are you this morning?"

"Fine."

He cleared his throat. "So look, I've got some things to do this morning."

Well, this was awkward. "Uh. Okay. I'm on the phone with Poppy. Can I call you back?"

Dan barked, "You should ask her about that photo with Pappineau. And tell her about Shep. Ask her about the Circus thing. And, Caesar, brace yourself, but your little blondie is broke. She's not making payroll. Money makes people do crazy things."

"I have to go. We'll talk later."

I hung up. This new day was turning to crap. I clicked my phone, but Poppy was gone, and she didn't pick up again.

From the back room Nan called, "You need to drop about ten quarters in that cuss jar, Caesar."

I took the bus into Manhattan. The sun was shining, the trees were trembling in the spring breeze, the smog was thick, and I was tempted to go back to the gallery. I squelched that impulse. I had my lunch money in my pocket with my cell phone, and a crisp resume printed on good paper in my messenger bag. I figured, if nothing else, I looked damn fine in my new Diesel jeans.

The Albright Gallery was uptown, near the big museums and close to Central Park. The real estate alone gave it clout, but the Albright name lent the gallery serious influence. I guess if I was going to be anyone's assistant, Mallory would be the one.

It was ten, I'd called Stephanie and she encouraged me to stop by early. So I was halfway down 73rd Street, nearly to the side entrance where the offices were located, when Jean Luc Pappineau and Mallory exited the building in a huff. I stopped dead in my tracks when Shep appeared behind them in a breathtakingly expensive cashmere blazer in the exact shade of his eyes. He had on another pair of two hundred dollar jeans and those silly boots.

Jean's hands gesticulated theatrically. Mallory's narrow face was set in her usual smooth, dignified lines. She didn't look impressed with Jean, no surprise there. Shep followed them in what I read as obedience. I didn't trust him. And I was more confused than ever. What the hell was he doing here?

They didn't see me, possibly they didn't recognize me dressed as a normal gay. The trio turned briskly and headed toward Park Avenue. I followed them. I mean, why not? I needed to speak to Mallory and Jean and...I was curious enough to spy. I hustled to catch them, but they had a quarter-block lead. They walked as if they were late for an appointment. It was ten thirteen.

I jogged when they turned the corner, heading south. I was nearly there, but slowed when Jean Luc stopped dead on the sidewalk. He said, "You can't pull from this show. I already announced it."

"You were premature. I lost my assistant this morning and a few things have come up."

"You owe me this show. I had to suffer through a lot of bullshit all spring. You told me it was a go."

Mallory laid it out. "Schumacher pulled his funds. Until I can deal with this"—she nodded to Shep crisply—"my hands are tied. If you'd like to attend our meeting, fine, but you need to be circumspect, Jean. Please."

Shep was going to use his clout with Chad to save the day for Mallory? Why? He didn't even like real art. He bought prints from Pottery Barn. Mallory's heels clicked on the pavement. People moved from her path. Pappineau was leaping around like a monkey to follow her, his hair blowing in big chunks around his head. Shep took his iPhone out and fiddled with it. "You should offer a reward for that painting. I bet someone would turn it in."

Jean clapped Shep on the back. "That's my boy! Good thinking."

They turned into an office building where a liveried doorman let them in. The three disappeared. This must be the base of Chad's empire.

I went back to the museum to drop off my resume and grill Mallory's assistant. Stephanie sat at her desk, filing. Her neat office was right outside Mallory's. "Hey, Steph. How did it go this morning?"

A scrappy go-getter from the south Bronx, Steph was a narrow-waisted, bone-thin woman of color who didn't take shit from anyone, except Mallory. She modeled her dress on her stylish boss—pencil skirt, tailored blouse, minimal jewelry. It seemed a pity that the two of us spent most of our time hiding our personalities for such a small reward. "'Bout as you'd expect. She sucked on her teeth and smiled. I gave her two weeks."

I handed her my resume. "I had hoped to see her, but she left with Pappineau and, uhm, was that Shep McNamara?"

She nodded. "He came with Pappineau to make nice for Mallory. Huh. What do you think of that Pappineau guy? Cuz he's a royal pain in my ass. Boss called me Saturday all set to have this damn show, and now she's pulling the plug. You know how much work I did over the weekend?"

"Yeah. I do know. Firsthand."

"Mmph. That's just so typical. These art people are nuts." She scoped me out. "You look nice. Them Diesel jeans?"

I nodded. "My cousin has a friend in the garment district."

"Nice."

"So, does Mallory do that a lot? Pull out of shows?"

"She's crazy. Look, this gig pays better than most, but I'm sick of it. My best friend from City College got a job for Delta. She's a flight attendant. I think I'd rather serve peanuts and show people how to click together a seat belt than do this. And it pays better. Plus it has benefits. Dental."

Flight attendant? She was thin enough. "Well, tell her I dropped this off. Steph, do you know why she hasn't paid Posh Nosh? I mean, is everything all right here? I don't want to be in a situation where I don't get paid. I need to move forward, you know?"

"She didn't get all her grant money. It's the economic downturn, I guess. She started acting all bitchy after the last show, and then her nephew walks in the other day, and suddenly my computer is his computer. I'm telling you: I'm outta here. I'm gonna fly me some friendlier skies."

"Ncphew?"

"Yeah. Good-looking man, but nosey. You'd like the look of him. He's like Gerard Butler hot. Tall, dark, handsome. Muscly. Mmmm-mm. But he was fucking around with my files. Sticking his nose in my drawers. Asking me questions. Looking at my mailing lists. I don't like that Mr. Dan Man."

Dan? Mallory had a nosy nephew named Dan. Dan? I blinked to clear my thoughts. It could not be.

"That's him right there." She nodded toward Mallory's desk. I peeked in the doorway. Why was I worried? There were a million nosy, computer-literate Daniels in New York City. I crept into Mallory's smart office on my tiptoes. What the hell was the matter with me? I'd been in here before. I manned up and turned the tiny Tiffany frame on her desk. It was a photo of two men together on a fishing boat. They both wore floppy hats and ugly vests. I'd had mind-blowing sex with the one on the left.

I started coughing. Wheezing. Choking again.

"Hey, you okay? You don't look good, Ce."

I struggled to find my breath. "Hhhh...haaa..."

"You need a lozenge? I'll get you some water." Steph dashed to the cooler. Trapped by her narrow skirt, she took rapid baby steps across the office while I stared at the photo of my new pal. She poured me a paper funnel of water and toddled quickly back. I downed water gratefully, my vision blurred.

I wiped my mouth with the back of my hand. "Dan Green is Mallory's nephew?"

"Green? Who's Green? His name is Albright."


I don't recall saying goodbye. No. What I remember is hitting the door so hard the metal frame knocked the iron railing with a clang. I cleared the door, hopped the stairs and pounded down the sidewalk with my phone against my ear. People passed me, making way, as I plowed through pedestrian traffic like a human steamroller. Who the hell was Dan Albright? What did he gain by lying to me? He certainly had plenty of time to divulge this tiny detail before last night. That bastard.

The phone rang and rang—at last Dan's voice mail picked up, and I heaved into the phone, "Albright? Albright? At what point were you going to tell me that? *Albright?*"

I snapped my phone shut. That went slightly better than I'd anticipated. I walked, sinking down to catch the subway—the sunshine no longer of any interest to me. I wanted to burrow like a mole into the underground and nurse my black temper. I called Peter before I lost service and said, "I'm sorry to inform you that today I quit."

I shut my cell phone again and took the yellow line downtown toward NYU. I needed to think, and what better place to organize one's thoughts than on a stuffed New York subway car?

Since Jean Luc and Mallory weren't going to have their show, I wasn't going to worry about finding Justin Timberlake by Wednesday. Scratch that right off the top of the list. I still had his ear on my dresser with that floral wire and hot glue. Now it was Peter's problem. As was Mallory's missing painting— which my gut told me Peter had stolen from her because *he was an asshole.* He'd disappeared. Screw him and the little clown car he rode in on. Served him right someone took the damn thing from him.

Shep. He had a connection with Jean Luc—I could imagine exactly what kind. He'd probably come to the gallery Friday night to see him, not me. Maybe he'd hooked up with someone at the party—and he was more embarrassed than upset. Maybe it was Jean he was keeping secrets from, not the public, or Chad, or that yellow-toothed Estelle. I'd advised him to call the police on numerous occasions and he'd declined, so I owed him nothing.

As far as Rachel went? My guess was that anyone who had seen Rachel's private area would know the truth about her...him...her and be confused or angry. I think. I wasn't too clear on the logistics of hermaphroditism. Why would anyone want money from her? Anger. Jealousy. Revenge. All the usual suspects. She'd been in the office with Peter. For all I knew, she had taken that horrible painting.

And finally, the Circus of Despair. Now there was a title that summed up this entire weekend. Mallory hired her nephew to investigate. Fine. *Dandy*. I wasn't guilty of anything but promiscuity and premature ejaculation. The painting had nothing to do with me.

What mattered most was that my very best friend was in financial trouble. She needed to be saved—I moved that into my Shit To Do column.

I was so angry, my teeth hurt. People were cutting me a wide berth in the full subway car. I was grumbling and grousing to myself, my hands flailing. I was muttering in Italian. I considered calling Cousin Joey, but I had no definitive plan.

We stopped near Washington Square, and I marched back into the daylight by rote. I didn't know why I was walking toward the gallery, but I guess that's where my feet wanted to take me. I was nearing Denali's Deli, when Brandon Wakefield stepped out of the doorway, his face ablaze, his hat low and his lips stretched like a lamprey. I had completely forgotten about him. Arrested, I stood there wide-eyed and repulsed. He was working a lime popsicle with his swollen mouth. "Holy fuck, Bran, what happened to you?"

"Hey, Theethar. Whad ahe you doin' here?"

"I'm quitting my job. Are you...well? Can I help you?"

He sucked on his pop, shaking his head. "No. I hag anoder praceedure."

"You let someone do that to you on purpose? You paid them?" He looked like an overfilled sausage. His skin was still vibrantly red from the chemical peel, but his lips? Maybe when the swelling went down they'd be considered bee-stung. I squinted. Tiny threads were barely visible at his temples. "What's wrong with your eyes?"

"Stithes. I hag werk. Theetar. I keepth thelling you."

"Oh. So this will all make you look younger when it heals?" Lord save us from the hands of Father Time. And Dr. Mengele-Bronner. I was beginning to think looking like my father wasn't such a bad thing. He'd aged splendidly. Maybe if I took after Tino or Vito...

"'es. Be bedder in a week." He was looped on painkillers, his pupils the size of pennies. He blinked innocently at me, the drugs and the stitches making him appear even more slow-witted than normal.

"Bran. I need to ask you, flat out, did you take anything from the gallery Friday night?"

He blinked slowly again. "Jus the twuck. And futh you, Theethar."

"I know. I'm sorry to ask, it's just...stuff is missing."

"There'th alwayth thomething mithing."

I helped Brandon, stoned and stumbling, into a cab. It seemed his Dr. Bronner was in the Village and practicing his craft daily on the aging Brandon. Hopefully practice did indeed make perfect. Jeez.

At Starbucks I decided to order a macchiato, calories be

damned. I needed a fix. I was running around half-cocked, which was no way to run, and I required sugar. Sugar was the key to good mental health. I waited in line craving whipped cream, but before my turn came, a hand gripped my shoulder, scaring the wind out of me.

"Jesus."

"Hey." It was Rachel, smiling broadly. "I thought that was you."

"Hey, yourself." She was as adorable as ever, in a skintight sundress with a matching jacket. Everything today was hot pink and teal blue. She had parrots hanging from her ears, and a knobby bead necklace buried in her tits. She looked like Mae West ready for Key West. "How'd it go? Any news?"

"I was just going to call you. You'll never guess who I saw."

"After today? Probably not."

"Brandon."

"Really? I saw him too—"

"I had to work today, at Nosh. I've been running errands all morning for Poppy, and I think it's Brandon. He was the last one out. He could have taken the head thing in the oven with him. The oven. It was big enough, right? Well, guess who is looking bee-stung and like he's been at ground zero of a supernova? Brandon. He had *work.*"

"I know. Oh my God. He looks like a walking knockwurst. Don't you all have a gig? He's like Frankenstein's more attractive younger brother."

"Poppy won't let him serve looking like that. But, Ce. Listen. This blackmail person, he wants four hundred from me, right?"

I followed Rachel's conversational leaps with relative ease, which was unnerving. "Yeah. And five grand from me, eight something from Shep, and God knows what from Peter."

"So I see Brandon and I think, hey, when I had that collagen last year? It was four hundred, you know? So I says to myself, I says: What's it cost to have one of them peels? And it's eight hundred something, Ce. I looked it up on my phone." She waved her iPhone at me. I really needed to get one of those. "You know what that means?"

"I have no idea." My attention shifted to the seductive display inside the confectionary case. It was my turn to order. "Caramel macchiato, venti, extra syrup, whipped cream, no foam. And one of those cupcakes." I pointed vaguely to the case. The sales associate wisely grabbed the biggest dessert item they had without bothering me for further input. I'd earned this. I'd burned it off in Daniel Albright's bed last night. My stomach growled.

*"I'm taking you for a ride on my bike tomorrow,"* he'd said when I left. Before he'd kissed me again and I'd melted against him like the butter in that fucking cupcake.

He'd taken me for a ride, all right. *Albright.* I snatched the bag from the Starbucks boy's hand, nearly taking his fingers off in my rush to get my treat.

"That'll be eight fifty."

"Eight?" I squeaked. I counted my change with care.

Rachel chattered on with enthusiasm. "I think he's getting all of us to pay for his surgery. I figured it all out. Cuz Brandon? I used to go with him. And Shep would do him. I mean that guy is a total whore." She was impossibly pleased with herself.

"Brandon or Shep? Brandon's straight. What do you mean?"

"Shep. He's slept with one of Poppy's boyfriends. He's just a whore. I mean, it's one thing to like boys, like I do; it's another

148

to be an asshole about it."

I took my drink from the overworked coffee slave. "Back up a second, Rach. You think Brandon is blackmailing everyone he knows to pay off his plastic surgeon?" Christ, it was crazy enough to be true. "And what? He's got us on some kind of sliding scale? How he thinks that I have more money than Peter is...but maybe you're on to something. I just asked him and he said no. Maybe he lied."

Rachel's painted mouth slackened. "You think?"

"Yeah. Well, he's on painkillers now, probably not the best time to confront him. I'll check into it, though. Just don't say anything, okay? I'll figure it out. Did the person contact you again?"

"Not yet, but he will. Oh, I know it's him. He's not the brightest crayon in the shed."

"Uhm. Right."

Brandon. I could go knock on his door and get our shit back. Tell him we could pretend this whole thing had never happened. He wasn't a bad guy, you know? He was sort of harmless. And right now? He wasn't exactly fleet of foot. But if he'd taken Poppy's money? That was another matter. That was Joey territory.

Rach swung her ass out of the Starbucks, every eye in the joint focused on the swish of her skirt. She was something. And actually, she was on to far more than Detective Dan *Albright* was.

I sipped my goody. Whipped cream coated my lip, and I hit the street, wandering, wondering what to do next when a bus rolled past. Shep McNamara smiled with charming crocodile teeth from its side. His face was bloody huge. *Mr. Potter's Lullaby Coming This Summer! Thursdays at 8:00!* Letters a foot high. I scalded my tongue on the coffee. Shep was so handsome, those candy devil eyes, the platinum hair, the Crest White, cheeky smile. I had this very minute spent my last eight dollars on a cupcake, and he was a goddamn transit billboard, selling a lie at God-knows-what price.

I sucked at my whipped cream, licked chocolate mocha frosting from my cupcake—my oral fixation was out of control as I chewed my feelings into submission. I knew what I was going to do next, and like this less-than-virtuous lunch, I'd probably regret it.

# Chapter Nine:
# Coconut Shrimp

Nana and I sat on the couch in her living room, suffering through the purgatory that was *Mr. Potter's Lullaby*. Nan had been kind enough to make us both popcorn, but my blood sugar was still in orbit from my earlier binge. Besides, I wasn't watching this dreck for entertainment purposes; I had to know what Shep had signed on for.

Nana threw a handful of popcorn at the TV. "This was your first boyfriend? What a waste. Such a fine-looking man. I didn't know he'd found religion."

On the screen, Shep rode a horse through a bucolic pasture in some unnamed Appalachian hill town. Tall meadow grasses parted like the Red Sea in his wake. He had a Stetson angled rakishly on his handsome head, and on his feet, those cowboy boots. This explained the new look.

"They could at least jazz it up with musical numbers, or some sex. Maybe they could have done a Baywatch Bible Hour, because this is weak. He does look good in those jeans, though."

He did look good in those jeans, then again, he'd look good in a bread bag. "I know." What else could I say? She was right.

*Mr. Potter's Lullaby* was discordant. Gorgeous cinematic

detail flattened by lead-fisted melodrama of biblical proportion. Missionary Potter rode handsome and upright from town to town delivering the good news. In the two-hour pilot, Shep taught a valuable lesson to a "sexually confused" teenager. A lesson that had little semblance to the kind of discipline Shep seemed to prefer, I might add.

It appeared to be aimed at young people. No wonder Shep was terrified. It was like he was being held up as an example of What Not to Do While Acting in the Closet.

I was intensely uncomfortable with the direction he'd taken, because if asked, I wasn't going to lie for him about our past relationship. I might not broadcast it, but I wasn't hiding. I'd done it for three years, and I wouldn't hide or lie for anyone ever again.

I sat rigidly in my chair, biting my back teeth and squeezing the puff right out of handfuls of popcorn. He should have turned this role down.

Nana hit me with a piece of popcorn. "Pumpkin, you need to lighten up. Get out more. Find a new guy. Someone who's got a little pride."

I smiled at her. "That's a good thought. Next time I need to go for substance and not style."

Shep mangled another stiffly written line while clutching some scantily clad, loose woman to his manly chest.

Nan said, "He had more chemistry with that young boy."

"I can't watch this anymore."

"Do you realize what's going to happen to him if he doesn't come clean? He's going to make a lot of people very angry." She was a shrewd lady, my grandmother.

"Nana. He's killing himself. The best thing he could do for his career is to come out before this gets big. Come out, come out wherever you are. He'd get good press. He should have held out for a show that sent a positive message. Instead he's prostituting himself for Pottery Barn." I was gearing for a full-blown rant. "Because this kind of exposure is dangerous. He's demeaning himself." No wonder he was terrified. I was feeling militant. I needed to find my Harvey Milk T-shirt and go camp outside Shep's apartment with a sign: *Burst down those closet doors once and for all, and stand up and start to fight.*

This shit was wrong, and I was ashamed of myself for having once loved him.

I went to the kitchen, utterly depressed by that uplifting festival of homophobia, and the doorbell rang. That was weird. No one came to the house. "I got it."

Not that Nana was about to miss a second of Shep's snug-fitting, jean-clad sermon on the mount.

I opened the door, six o'clock Monday evening, the sun setting, the pigeons roosting on the ledges, and Dan Albright stood on Nana's doorstep with a scowl on his face and those shades covering his eyes. He had a shiny black helmet under his arm, which he thrust into my stomach with a *wop*. "Put this on. We're going for a ride."

I slapped it back into his gut. "No, Mr. Albright. Go screw yourself." I would have said *fuck* but I didn't have another quarter for the jar.

I tried to slam the door, but he stuck his boot in the threshold and held the front door open with his palm.

"Everything all right, Caesar?" Nana called from the living room. "You're missing tears."

"I'm fine," I called. I said to Dan, "Isn't this police brutality, Detective?"

Dan pointed at my sock-covered feet. "C'mon. Grab your goddamn shoes, and let's go. We need to talk."

153

"Why?"

"Because you turned off your phone. I have work to do, you know. You're being a pain in my ass."

"*Excuse me?*"

He sighed. "I need to talk to you about Poppy. We can have this fight later. Please. I need your help."

That was the magic word. Not please, but Poppy. I waved goodbye to Nana who was hooting into her popcorn, slid on some loafers and grabbed a cardigan—purposely seeking the most ridiculous wishy-washy attire to wear on Dan's beefy man-cycle.

He smiled like he was forgiven. "You are such a feisty thing."

"And you are such an arrogant dick. I'm not doing this for you."

He stuck the helmet on my head and dragged me into the street. "Mount up."

"Excuse me?"

Dan climbed on and I tentatively *mounted up*, two pissed-off fellahs, ready to hit the open road on a suicide machine. "Are you able to drive? I've never actually been on a motorcycle before."

"What? How is that possible?"

"I just...don't...like to...they're dangerous. I prefer cabs, the subway, walking."

"You know, you're a wuss. You're so lively on the outside, but inside, you're scared of the entire world. What's up with that? Live a little. Take a fucking chance."

I swallowed hard. His casual comment was painfully astute.

"Just hang on. Close your mouth so you don't get bugs,

and keep your big Italian feet where they belong."

"Fine. But I don't like this."

"Noted, Romano." He ooched forward, or whatever it is that one does on a bike, his long legs walking the two of us into traffic, and then we were off. Sort of. It was loud, and we stopped fairly often, merging here and there. Dan guided us with painstaking effort through the Monday gridlock until, at long last, wind in our hair, we moved up a single block. This is why I take the subway.

We crawled toward Manhattan. I was clueless as to why. I just sat there, feeling my nuts vibrate, checking out the city as it made its breathtaking transition from day to evening, and trying to keep my fingers from circling Albright's beefy neck.

He relaxed back, his thick body between my spread knees, one hand on his thigh as we crossed the bridge. He should drive with two hands, shouldn't he? That was alarming. But I was going to do this if it killed me, which come to think of it, it might.

Most of the traffic was flowing away from the city, so we had a clear stretch across the bridge when Dan hit the throttle and cold air blasted me. I curved against his back, the smell of leather and cardamom and smog mixing together, and stole warmth from Dan's body.

It was sort of invigorating and, for the first time since last night, when Dan last led me into thrilling new territory, I enjoyed myself. I was flying again.

Until I realized we were headed uptown. "Where are we going?"

"Shep's apartment."

My knuckles tensed around his shoulders. I flexed my fingers. I was going to strangle him when I got off this thing.

155

It took twenty-five minutes to drive four miles up the FDR. It was nearly seven when we pulled to a stop a block from Shep's building. The streetlights were on, and I was freezing. "You should have told me to wear a jacket."

"And spoil your snit? No way. I have one in my saddlebag for the trip back. Calm down."

"Stop saying that to me. I'm not going up there. I just watched his miserably antigay Mr. Potter, and I'm liable to gut him with a ballpoint pen."

"Caesar. I need you to be the bad cop. Do you hear me? You can be as pissed as you want, that'll work. Take your aggression out. Neuter him. I don't care. I need Shep to load this software on his computer."

"Why?"

He said flatly, "Because the PayPal account Mallory was told to use this morning? It's Poppy's."

I swallowed.

"I want to see if Shep's being blackmailed by the same person. And Rachel. Because you asked me to help you. Okay? I'll be good cop. It certainly worked yesterday."

I wanted to trust him. I did. "Fine. As long as you know that I'm only doing this for Poppy." In the elevator, I tucked in my shirt and ran my fingers through my hair. "Do I have helmet head?"

"A little. But I like those jeans. Your ass is beautiful. Tight. I'd like to taste it again."

"That's out of the question."

He laughed.

We made it to Shep's door and Dan said, "Look. I'm sorry about this thing. I lied. I had to. And then there didn't seem to be a good time to tell you."

"Really? How convenient for you to tell me right here. That's not good enough."

Dan smiled his smug, knowing smile. He stepped close. His rough finger soothed my neck, right where I had a noticeable bite. I remembered his mouth there, his beard burning, his tongue, and my flesh sizzled under his touch. He leaned in, and his lips hovered a hairsbreadth away from my whiskered skin. He whispered, "It is good enough, baby. You're just being difficult."

My stomach dropped, and instinctively I turned my mouth toward his. He was so close, so warm, so—

Shep ripped the door open, eyes blazing. Dan took his time moving away from me. This was his idea of good cop?

"What the hell are you doing here? You can't be here." Shep stepped into the hall dressed in...was that Armani?

Dan crowded him, a police tactic that worked, because Shep stepped back and just like that, we were standing in the cavernous foyer. It took me only a moment to realize we'd walked into a dinner party. There were about fifteen people that I could see. Light jazz played over the sound system. I heard a cork pop.

Dan shot me a look. "Change of plan." He pumped Shep's hand and gave a hearty, "Hey, Sheppard. We were in the neighborhood again and, well it's crazy, but I said to Caesar, we should drop by and say hello. Since we're here."

Estelle Rosenstein clopped in. "Mac? Everything okay?" Her eyes widened, then narrowed, on me—you know, *the stupid thing Shep had done in college.*

"We were...we're...we...are...are...I..." I was the worst bad cop on the force. I stumbled and stuttered like a fourth-grade spelling bee dropout.

Shep's attention darted between us. His color was much

better today, but perspiration beaded his forehead. "Estelle. Why don't you see to our guests? This will only take a sec."

From down the hall, over the music and the cocktail laughter, I heard a soft voice say, "Coconut shrimp?"

I knew that voice. I shoved Shep out of my way, my hand sliding on silk, and wandered toward the dining room. Stylishly dressed people milled around, sipping from cut-crystal tumblers full of pale liquor and tall glasses of what had to be fine Merlot. The gas fireplace was lit, the apothecary cabinet was spread with dainty, colorful hors d'oeuvres, and Poppy stood by a club chair with a tray of coconut shrimp in one hand and a handful of ivory-colored napkins in the other. Her headband was puce, her dress yellow, and she looked positively green around the gills. Chad Schumacher tossed a shrimp tail onto her platter and smiled icily. He gave her a dismissive look and turned to his horse-faced wife. Poppy's smile flattened. She did not like that man, and rightly so.

"Poppy?"

Startled, she turned her pale eyes on me. "Ce? What are you doing?" She came wearily across the dining room, and every few steps, she swallowed grimly. She held that shrimp plate on a straightened arm, apparently to keep the smell away. I swear she was ready to vomit.

"I'm just...we're...we..."

A real smile lit her eyes. "Slow down."

I nodded and took a deep breath. "Are you all right?"

Estelle came clopping back into the dining area. "Well, I guess everyone knows everyone."

I said without thinking, "What a happy coinci—"

"Not me." Dan strode in with his arm slung around Shep's shoulder in a friendly chokehold. He took in Poppy's color, my nervous comment, Estelle's accusing looks and Chad's zealot eyes. "I'm Daniel Albright. I'm Caesar's lover."

Everyone turned to stare at me. I'd never seen so many tonsils in my life. Poppy dropped the shrimp platter. She covered her mouth—not to sick up, but to stop her giggles.

"I thought your name was Green," Shep said, unable to hide his confusion.

"Dan," I gritted out. "Behave."

He flung a hand to the Nazi. "Name's Albright. Daniel Albright, from the Baxter Miller Albrights of Westchester? Perhaps you know my Uncle Riley?"

Riley Albright, the State Senator. Hm. And a Democrat. Now that was hitting Chad where it hurt. I was certainly impressed. Chad Schumacher unwillingly shook Dan's hand. "I'm familiar. I know Mallory. I think your uncle and I play golf."

"Doubtful, but hey, if you say so."

I coughed into my hand. Here was yet another personality of Detective Dan's. This one was outrageously self-possessed. He stood taller, he smiled broadly, he was confident and he owned the room. Dan played his heritage like a trump card. Yup. He was a total asshole. Even Shep stood in his shadow. I was mad at Dan, but I couldn't help but be amused by this incarnation. Honestly? My heart softened a smidge.

"So I just need to steal our friend Sheppard for a moment, and then we'll be out of your hair. Caesar and I have some things we need to do." He winked at me slow and sexy and, I can't believe this, but I think I blushed.

Poppy said quietly, "So this is Detective Dan? I like him much better than the last one. Look at you. You're all bitten up."

I bent down and helped her pile fallen shrimp onto her

plate. "Who are these people?"

"The money for Shep's show. These are his new owners. He's going to kill you for coming here. He's been screeching all day about me keeping my lips zipped. He's scared. If I didn't need this job, I'd have cancelled."

The two of us walked into the kitchen. Rachel was wearing another crazy frock—this one covered in vulgar cherries. She was standing at Shep's six thousand dollar Jenn-Air range basting a leg of lamb. Pots burbled. I saw baby carrots. Asiago and sage scalloped potatoes. My stomach made a noise. The smell of Pish Posh's Port Wine and Rosemary Roasted Lamb filled the kitchen, and I salivated. It was my absolute favorite.

Rachel grinned when she saw me. "Hey. What are you doing here?"

"Just visiting."

Poppy found a saltine and two Perriers. She stuffed a lime into mine. "Rach, could you go serve? I'm about ready to puke." She handed me a drink and we clinked bottles. "To your new *lovah*. Oh my God. He's fucking brilliant. Tell me he's as good in bed. That was worth this entire horrible month, Ce. I love you."

I moved closer to the cutting board, where two tied boneless beauties cooled. "I love you too. I love this lamb more. Dan's fucking with Shep to get some information for Mallory Albright. He's not a fan." I tried to pick a tiny piece of lamb from the end.

"Mmmhmm, I'll bet. But that man? He likes you. No hiding it." She went to work getting the food in order, ever set on her goal. She sliced me a sliver of savory meat. It melted in my mouth.

Poppy swallowed again tightly.

"You don't look good. Should you be working?"

"I've been sick all day. Nerves. I spent yesterday with my parents."

"What did your dad say?"

"He said I told you so, and he'd see. The market's not good."

The kitchen door opened and Shep tripped in. He was having trouble with those fancy shoes. I blinked, because through the door, Jean Luc Pappineau stood hobnobbing with the Schumachers. Jean's hair was as unkempt as ever, but he was decked in finery and dazzling.

"I thought you said this was all backers?"

"It is."

"Why's Jean here?"

Shep raked a hand through his platinum hair and said to me, "You have to leave. I'm not trying to be rude. But—"

Poppy's knife came down on a hunk of lamb. Steam curled around her hand. She ignored her cousin. "He's Shep's guest. I'm sure they could enlighten us both as to why he's here. Trying to find his own backer, maybe? Maybe he's here as someone's date. You watch out for that man." She pointed at me with the blade. "He's got issues."

Shep blasted me. "Please, Caesar. I need you to go. I can't concentrate with you here—"

"Are you kidding me—?"

"I'm working." He threw his hands in the air. "I'm sorry I came to the gallery Friday. Yes. I get it. I'm sorry. Please. Everyone here is relying on me...Estelle, Jean, Poppy, Chad. I can't fuck this up. Okay? Take that boyfriend of yours with you. I let him do what he asked. I have to deal with these people."

Poppy agreed with her cousin. "You should go. We'll hook up later. I have to work. And damn it, where's my truck?"

"Shit. I'm sorry. It's at Nan's."

Dan appeared at the door. "Ready, babe?"

That was laying it on a bit thick.

"Sort of." I hugged Poppy hard. She was skin and bones. "You need to eat something."

She nodded. "Okay, okay. Don't crap your pants. Just leave. I'm fine."

# Chapter Ten:
# Monday Night at Rocco's

I liked the bike because parking was so easy. We found a spot half a block from Rocco's and walked down the dark side of the street to see my father. I told Dan I wanted ravioli.

He was fiddling with his BlackBerry. Occasionally he'd mutter, "Dr. Bronner charges seven seventy-five for Botox." And, "It's twelve hundred bucks to have a lunchtime lift. He sticks barbed thread in your forehead and knots it. Says here it takes less than an hour."

"That's what he had done. That's barbaric. What costs five thousand dollars?"

He diddled with his thumbs. "Breast augmentation."

I stewed quietly as we walked the block. I seemed to be stuck with Dan this evening, and I was still unclear about the whole Albright business. I was wrapped in his warm, spare jacket. It smelled just like him, but it was too big. "It's Brandon. I've thought so from the get-go. He works for Poppy, he's orange, he could easily blackmail Shep for having sex with one of Nosh's staff, he needs money, and he's had his finger in everyone's pie. Including Rachel's." I shuddered.

"Except for Peter's."

"We don't know that. Peter hasn't called me since I quit this morning."

Dan's brow lifted without any medical assistance. "You didn't tell me that. That's bold. You good with that?"

"I guess I'll have to be. Look, it's Brandon. We should just go over there right now. He's probably knocked out on OxyContin."

He shook his head. "No. Not going to happen. I'll check his place tomorrow."

"Why? You've dragged me everywhere else."

"Shep is a pussy. You could take him down with a finger. I think he's a victim, and he's a lead. Brandon? He's another story. Let me handle this."

"You didn't have any problem with me earlier."

"I needed you. I appreciate you wanting to do this, but you ever spent any time with real criminals? Like up there at Manhattanville? Anyone pushed far enough to commit a felony?"

I swallowed, thinking of my uncles. "Uh."

"That's what I thought. We don't really know Brandon, and he's desperate. He may have raped Shep."

"No way."

"I'll handle it, Caesar. You just keep your tight little ass out of trouble—"

What a dick. I'd go anyway.

"—I know you want to protect Poppy."

"Well, it's not Poppy. She has no reason to hurt me. And she doesn't have a penis. She didn't rape anyone, least of all her cousin."

"You never know. Look at Rachel."

"That's not funny."

It was only when we entered Rocco's that I recalled it was the first Monday of the month. My hale and hearty Uncle Tino met us at the door, a huge smile lighting his face, the entire clan behind him. The Gathering. Oh no. It was cocktails and supper—Romano style.

"We're not staying for supper," I hissed at Dan.

"Whatever you want."

"Caesar!" The bald head of my Uncle Tino gleamed almost red against the restaurant décor. My father insisted crimson velvet made the place look more authentic, but we all knew it was unflattering to those of a ruddy complexion. Shep had looked like a Martian.

Tino yanked me into a hug with gorilla-like arms. "*Ciao!*"

He whacked my back.

"Oof. *Ciao*, Tino." As tradition dictated, I kissed his cheek. He smelled like family: Aqua Velva and cigars. I bet he had a pocketful of quarters and a stogie in his jacket. I prepared myself for more backslapping, cheek kissing and pungent aftershave.

He let me go with a smile. His suit was creased and his tie too skinny. As the oldest son, my Uncle Tino sported my grandfather's flashy pinky ring. It twinkled on his fat finger. Tino's smile faltered. "Who's the cop?"

I'd brought a lawman into the place, and my uncle had ferreted the man's vocation in ten seconds. Detective Dan, Mr. Big Dick. I didn't know what to say.

Dan stepped up to the plate and shook his hand. "Dan Albright."

Tino's mouth flattened. He slashed at the air with his meaty hands. "You bringing a cop to the family supper, Caesar?"

"He's not a cop. He's a...friend."

Tino watched him with a slanted eye. "If you say so."

"*Ciao*, Caesar!" My cousin Joey arrived, his black hair tamed with product. We were the same age, but Joey was swarthier. He was wiry and wiggly and sharp as a blade. He shook my hand and stared with open curiosity at Dan. I'd never brought anyone to the restaurant, man or woman, since Shep. Except Poppy, of course. I bet you can figure out why.

"Wow. That's quite a large medallion. Is it new?" I needed to keep Joey from asking any questions.

"You like? I can get you one at cost."

"I'll think about it." I'd have to work on my upper-body strength to carry that much gold without straining myself. Joey winked at Dan. Dan didn't wink in return. In fact, he looked like he was trying to match Joey to any number of most-wanted photos.

"Them jeans look good. You need anything else, you let me know."

Dan glanced at my possibly ill-gotten pants.

"*Grazie,*" I said.

"How's my Poppy?" Joey grinned widely. His appreciation of my best friend had never wavered.

I swallowed my lie. "Poppy? She's...she's...you know...she's good. I'll call you tomorrow. I think she needs a new accountant. She's having some trouble."

"What's a matter? I'll call her tonight. She's my girl. Nobody messes with my girl."

When I assured Poppy my family would take her under their collective wing, I'd been serious. I suspected they wanted to help her because, at the time, they also hoped I'd straighten out and get married. I never corrected them, so they'd fallen over themselves to get her going. That's not lying. Not really. And now? She was a Romano. At times, I thought she fit in better with this group than I did.

My father joined us, his accent long gone. His apron was in place. "I saw her last week. She looks beautiful, but skinny. Business is booming. She's a good girl. What are you doing here? You never come to see us on Monday. You got trouble?"

He just shook Dan's hand without a word. As if they'd met before. "Hello, Mr. Romano. I've come back to steal your veal scallopini recipe."

Talk about turning on the charm. It wasn't going to work. I shot him a cool look, and he winked back at me.

"I stopped by to talk to you, Pop. I've got...to go...see a movie," I ended lamely.

Everyone gawked at the two of us. "You finally got a boyfriend and he's a cop?" Joey asked. He nodded at my new leather jacket. "Gay cop? I didn't even know there was such a thing."

Dan gave him a hard smile. "They don't last long."

My father saved me. "Talk to me? Why? You need money?" His bushy eyebrows rose hopefully. I'd never take a penny from him; only the free food.

"Money! You need money? What's a matta? You knock someone up?" Paulie piped in. My brother had two plates in his hand and that white towel was still over one shoulder. I assumed it was fresh. "Isn't that gallery guy you're working for paying you?"

"No. No! I'm fine. I just need to talk to Pop for a minute." They were beginning to circle around me, eager to pry and assist. I searched for an out. My mother sat at the back booth quietly observing my discomfort. Her glance went between Dan and me. She was drinking a dry martini, as she did every time the family gathered. She was in her usual position, ignoring my sister-in-law and reading a *People* magazine. She raised her glass to me with a tiny, amused smile and went back to her gossip rag. Donna was on her cell phone. Her yellow hair was teased in a claw, and I knew my mother was secretly itching to take a comb to Donna's head. She'd wait to grill me in private.

"You in trouble?" Vito threw his arm around my shoulder and led me away from Dan to a faraway booth.

"Trouble? Me?"

"Maybe you sold some kind of fake art?" Tino added helpfully—almost hopefully.

"What? That's terrible. No. I...I...I...just need...I..."

Paulie said around a mouthful of peppercorn bruschetta, "Hup. There he goes again. He's gonna lie."

I snapped my mouth closed and flushed. Dan waited by the door reading a menu. He asked, "So we're not going to eat?"

My father slid into the vinyl booth. He sat across from me. "Everybody. Go away. Let me see what my son wants. He never asks for nothing from nobody."

Vito patted my cheek with his chubby hand. "You're a good kid. You let me know what I can do." He squinted meaningfully. "Anything at all." He stared at Dan.

I swallowed. "Sure, Uncle V. I will." A vision of Dan floating facedown in the East River flickered briefly through my mind. But Vito was just a simple business owner. He wasn't mob. Not really. "I'm good, though."

Pop let them go back to their food and their wives and their not-so-subtle perusal of my guest. "So. What's the problem? You need money, right?"

I sighed, thinking of Poppy. "Maybe. Right now? I need to ask you something."

His expression was serious. "Anything."

"I need to use the pick gun."

My father's hand snaked out and he smacked my head. "What are you thinking?"

"Ow!" The entire restaurant went quiet, the only sound Michael Bublé warbling over the speakers and Donna cluelessly chatting into her cell. I dropped my voice so the others couldn't hear. They were all on pins and needles, I was sure. Dan appeared to be choking. "Ouch. I'm just trying to get my property back."

"Then you'd ask this person for your things back. Something's wrong. What happened? Who's bothering you?"

"Pop. I just want to know if I can borrow the lock pick, and then I'll do this, get my stuff, and no one will be the wiser." I wasn't going to wait for Dan. I was sick of waiting on people.

My father was a good guy, but he was still my father. "You got trouble? We got trouble. You tell me who it is, and we'll get your stuff back for you. No questions asked."

"It's not like that."

His mouth turned mulish. My old man drummed his fingers on the table. "You tell me. Does this have anything to do with that Sheppard boy coming in here yesterday?"

How do parents do that?

"No...well...not exactly. Not really. Not that I know of." Lord stop me from talking.

"You can't even lie without fumbling. How you gonna do this? It takes skill." He pointed a thumb at Dan. "You got a cop right here. You ask him."

"I don't need anyone's permission. How hard can that thing be? Joey's been using it since he was eleven. Let me know. Call me later." I slid out of the booth. "I gotta go."

LB Gregg

Pop watched us. Hell, they all watched us leave—the passel of them sipping on their wholesale booze and single shot espressos. Ready to kill.

Dan dropped the menu on the counter. "So..."

I walked out into the street, Dan dogging my heels. I was tempted to go home with him, have some mind-blowing sex, and then...what?

I looked at my watch. "I need to get back."

"Caesar." He latched onto my sleeve and stepped me into the alley next to my father's restaurant.

I shook him off, but not angrily. "I'm still upset with you. I don't like lies. I know why you did. I understand you didn't want to...tip your hand. But you...and I...last night. That was...I've never really done that. And to find out I don't even know your name was harsh. I was with a liar for three years. Secrets are one thing, lies are another."

"Green is my mother's maiden name. She and Mallory were in college together. Did you see the house? It says Green on the fucking door, Ce. And I don't play games of secrets either. I left a career because I was supposed to keep secrets." He stroked my hair back from my forehead, pushing me, crowding me into the side of the building. Brick met my back, but not roughly. "I like you. I want to fuck you every time I see you. You're a loyal, smart, funny, honest, feisty little shit. You know what? I think you're making excuses. You're scared I'm going to hurt you, and you're finding a reason not to trust me."

Was I? I tried for smartass. "I don't know what you mean."

But he called my bluff. "Yes. You do." He kissed the underside of my jaw, and then he stepped back. "See you tomorrow, Romano. Stay out of trouble. I'll check Brandon first thing."

I waited, leaning against the wall, staring after him. I heard

170

his bike kick-start, and then he drove away, red taillight streaking down the block.

I went home. It was nine and I was damn tired. I showered. I shaved. I washed a load of clothes. I ate some ziti. I stared at Justin Timberlake's ear. I shut off my phone and then I lay down in my lonely, cold bed with my library book—which was overdue—and Nana's shedding overweight cat.

I was a spinster. It was official.

# Chapter Eleven:
# The Cupboard Under the Stairs

I had to return the van. Poppy left seven messages over the course of the night and early this morning. She said things like, "I'm sure you're getting the hot beef injection right now, but I need my fucking truck, Ce. Where are you?"

And:

"I had to use Rachel's brother's car. She was a total bitch about it. Where the fuck is my truck?"

And:

"Call me. Jesus. This is why it's unhealthy to not have steady orgasms with other people. Turn your phone on. I have to go to work."

And finally:

"Ce. I think someone is stealing from me, like skimming the till or whatever it's called. I think...that someone is trying to frame me...which is crazy, but Mallory Albright accused me flat out of taking some stupid painting of a lonely assed clown. As if I don't already live in a circus. She said she's hired someone to investigate me. I guess that's your new boyfriend, right? That's what you tried to tell me." Long pause. "I just...I think I need some help. I'm having a really bad day."

She wasn't answering her phone now. What the hell was

with these cell phones anyway? I was constantly at everyone's beck and call, but they were never at mine.

I pulled the van to a stop on a side street. Ostensibly, I was heading to Posh Nosh to deliver the delivery truck. That was the goal. Instead, I was parked in a well-preserved neighborhood of historic brownstones. They faced each other in neat rows, their steps swept clean, the front doors lacquered. It was eight forty in the morning, the main roads were choked with trucks and school buses, the sun was shining all sparkly on the dirty city, and I had Joey's lock-picking gun in my pocket. I was nervously reconsidering my options while sitting in the truck. This was probably a stupid idea.

I thought of Dan. He was going to be bent out of shape about this. But Brandon wasn't dangerous, he was a thief. Dan was the dangerous one. Albright. The name alone helped stiffen my resolve.

The phone rang. Peter had landed earlier. "I need you to come in," he said without even a hello. Three days he'd taken to call me back. "Where are you?"

"Right now? I'm in Park Slope. Didn't you get my message?"

"No. Look, I'll pay you overtime. Have you gotten any closer to finding the bust?"

"No, Peter, that's not my job. I think you need to come clean, call the insurance company, file a report with the police, tell Mallory you have a compulsion, let Pappineau know about his head, and start taking some responsibility for your own business."

"That's not possible."

Truer words were never spoken. I contemplated the skyline. "Look. I understand that you don't want to lose your reputation, but you're taking me down with you."

"I'll give you a raise."

I sighed, "No. Peter, I quit yesterday," and disconnected with the press of my thumb.

Another fifteen minutes slogged by, the sun heating the van. I was roasting in a long-sleeved Henley and a fresh pair of jeans. I took the tool out of my jacket pocket and remembered everything my cousin had said to me this morning. We'd had chocolate donuts and he'd taught me a new skill. Isn't family special?

My phone rang again. This time it was Jean. It was uncanny how these people thoughtlessly phoned me on my supposed day off. "Hello, Jean."

"What the fuck is going on over there?"

"Excuse me?"

From halfway up the street, Brandon stepped out of his brownstone and staggered down the steps. He appeared preoccupied, probably by his painful-looking face. He was even worse today; he looked monstrous.

"Mallory. She said we'd broken some kind of covenant. She thinks I put Peter up to taking some painting—and she pulled from the show. I had no idea what a lunatic she is. I've been fighting with her since yesterday. Kissing her ass and genuflecting for twenty-four hours. I want that show, Caesar, it's career making. Peter called and said there's been some kind of incident with one of the heads. I cannot handle another incompetent, you hear me? What the fuck is going on?"

Brandon raised his hand, waving at a passing taxi.

"How do you know Shep McNamara?"

"What? Why?"

"Humor me."

"You know anything about Shep?"

"Yes. I know more about Shep than most people alive. We

lived together for three years."

"Yeah. He told me something about that. So, the guy gives good head and likes to have his ass smacked."

"Well, that sums him up." In a neat little package tied with a bow. Apparently the word *discretion* wasn't on Shep's vocab list. He'd probably blown half of last night's guest list—and all of Poppy's staff. I could almost believe he'd had sex with Rachel. No wonder he'd been sweating.

Jean Luc surprised me when he admitted, "He's probably the most perfect date I've ever had."

Now that was news. "Where are you?"

"I'm on the subway, heading in."

"Listen. Has anyone asked you for money?"

He laughed humorlessly. "Everyone asks me for money. Even the IRS."

A cab pulled over and Brandon smiled, his lips stretching like rubber. He swayed on his feet. I said, "I'll call you back."

"Wait!"

I folded my phone and this time, I turned it off. Brandon and his cab merged into traffic and moved slowly toward the tunnel.

I got out of Poppy's van, dashed up the block and leaped the steps. This particular house was divided into three apartments, Brandon's place on the first floor. I slipped through the front door, and hoped to God I wasn't acting as conspicuously as I felt.

Brandon's door wasn't only unlocked, it was partially open.

"Hello? Anyone at home?" Nervously, I knocked. Who leaves the door open in New York? But I saw him leave. I stood there holding that foolish lock pick, and the door slid open on its own. It was a sign. The stairs twisting to the two apartments above were silent, so I pushed the door farther.

"Hell-oooo?" I sounded like one of the Golden Girls. I needed to stop that. I wasn't doing anything wrong. The door was unlatched, so, *technically,* I was simply checking to see if Brandon was all right.

I went into the hall, scoping his place out. It was long and narrow, as most brownstones are, the ceilings tall, the walls painted plaster, and Brandon's furnishings were incredible. All antique, all heavy, rich, masculine pieces that were fit for a king or a barrister. He must have inherited them from his Beantown kin, because these were beyond the reach of just about anyone. The dining room, living room, the hall coat rack, there were a few towering pieces crammed into the place. Here and there, the plaster revealed light rectangles where something once stood. He must have been reduced to pawning some of the family heritage.

Still, he was another single man with a large apartment. It used to be one of the perks of living across the river— affordability and space. Over these last ten years our real estate had gotten out of the hands of the locals. We were all scrambling to stay in neighborhoods which had somehow become prime real estate.

Anyway, the place had a long hall with doors all over the place. He should put numbers on them to keep track. What do we have behind Door Number One, Johnny?

Yes, I was nervous.

"Hello? Anyone at home?" Silence, and thank God for it.

I started flinging all the doors wide, peering in, and quickly shutting them. I was looking for booty. I checked the living room, dining room, bath, bedroom, and under the stairwell, yet another closet. Exactly like *Harry Potter.*

But no Justin Timberlake.

The apartment ended in a large open kitchen that stretched the entire width of the brownstone. It was the kind of kitchen you could raise a family in, with an island and view of a neat back alley. A door led to a tiny covered porch. Other than a pile of dishes in the sink, and an open bottle of Coca-Cola, there was nothing of interest. I kept searching.

I went back in the hall. My God. I'd never seen so many closets. There was a broom closet, a coat closet, a butler's pantry—

Something clattered in the hall, and I jumped like a jackrabbit into that stairwell closet. It was filled with winter clothing...and still no head or Mallory's lost painting.

Before panic overwhelmed me, the door swung open and Dan stepped into the closet. He covered my mouth with his hard hand. "Shhh. Someone's coming." He shut us in without a sound.

Heart in my throat, blood pounding through my temples, I stared at the shadowed outline of Dan, my eyes probably the size of golf balls. Where the hell had he come from? He was so close, I bet he could see veins throbbing in my skull. Bastard had scared the living hell out of me.

He leaned in, his lips nuzzling my ear. "You okay? I didn't mean to scare you, but you were about to get caught."

I had gotten caught, the idiot, by him.

I nodded. Dan did not see fit to move his hand from my mouth. I grabbed his wrist. Slits of light showed around the door's edge, and a small crack revealed itself behind Dan's right ear.

"You be quiet. It's Shep."

Shep? I nodded again and Dan moved his hand. I whispered against his ear, "If he opens this door, we're toast."

"No problem. I'll knock him out. I brought a taser."

I clutched his sleeve, feeling faint.

"I'm kidding, Caesar. All will be well. Until we leave and I smack you in the head."

I was so impossibly tense, my neck ached. Dan shuffled around, soundlessly slipping behind me so I could get a better view. Now I could see just enough to make me hyperventilate. I peeked out the crack, preparing for that moment when the jig was up. From here, I had a clear view of the kitchen doorway, the cabinets, and the hall on this end. That's all. From the other end of the apartment, the front door opened. Shep called, "Hello? Anyone home?"

The front door closed and I guessed that Shep was doing exactly what I had done. Looking around. For what? He couldn't retrieve a video. This entire scenario kept getting more confusing. Unless he was here to meet with Brandon, or confront him.

Doors continued to open and shut as he moved ever closer to our hiding place. It was only a matter of seconds before he jerked this one wide. I gripped the knob, thinking maybe I could hold it shut. And then, incredibly, there was another knock on the front door. It was damn quiet all of a sudden. I imagined Shep pissing himself in fear, and that brought an unwilling smile to my face. "Now who could that be?" Dan whispered.

"Hell if I know."

"Hello? Shep? I saw you go in here," Poppy called. The front door slammed and I jerked into Dan's arms. My best friend's voice was thin with anger. "What the hell are you doing here?"

She came snapping down the hall, *tap-tap-tap-tap*. Her blonde hair flipped past me as she stormed to the kitchen, muttering something about Joey telling her. I heard a distinct "Bran" and she disappeared.

There was a knock on the front door.

"Jesus." Dan was chuckling behind me. "You've got a parade following you."

"This isn't amusing. Get a grip on yourself."

His chin moved against my neck, and his arms slid around my waist, drawing me back. "I'd rather get a grip on you."

"*Yoooo-whoooo.*"

"Oh my God," I whispered, "that's Peter. How the hell did he find me so fast?"

Dan breathed against my ear. "You left Poppy's truck outside, Sherlock. Everyone is following you."

"He's not here. I don't know why I let you talk me into these things, Peter." I knew that cultured voice. It was Mallory. I wondered if my nana was close behind.

"I may have told Mallory where I was going, though," Dan murmured. "She and I spoke this morning. I'm surprised she's with Peter."

"Since we're here, we can just take a look. Hello?" Peter called out.

"We can't go in there." I'd never heard Mallory raise her voice before, not even to Jean Luc. She was as haughty as a queen, but there was an edge.

"Well, the door is unlocked." Those words were followed by the sound of a scuffle, then a hiss of breath. "Good God. I think that's him."

The door slammed and we listened as feet scampered into...I think the dining room. Maybe they would hide behind the drapes.

This was surreal. Ten minutes ago I'd been alone. Now there were six of us hidden in as many rooms.

The front door opened with a crack as it bounced against

179

plaster. "Yes. I'm sure. My temp is a hundred one. I've got the runs too. I don't feel right." Brandon passed the door in a blur of stretched, angry skin, going straight to the kitchen. Had he even noticed the door was unlocked?

I braced myself for his confrontation with Poppy, but nothing happened. She must be hiding in the microwave.

Dan's hand crept up from my waist. Was he hoping to calm me with his presence? He was having the opposite effect. I was strung as tight as a fiddle. His fingertips brushed the side of my arm. Startled, I flinched. "What are you doing?"

"Keeping you from going postal."

"You're doing it wrong." He kept stroking me like a cat. Embarrassingly, we'd explored each other enough two nights ago that my body responded at once. The long, dry spell had ended and I was hungry for hands on me. *His* hands. Although I'm sure he was pissed off to find me here. Maybe this was Dan's idea of punishment.

"No. I'm doing it right." His intentions anything but honorable, warm fingers delved under my shirt, tickling my navel. His words were barely audible. "I know you want it, Romano."

I swallowed. "Are you insane? This is not the time."

"You knew I was coming here. You wanted me to catch you. Admit it."

I shook my head.

He kissed the skin beneath my ear, his breath caressing me. "You love getting caught, Caesar. You wanted to get caught. And I've got you now."

Brandon's whining carried from the kitchen. "I think I need some antibiotics. It doesn't look right. I feel weird. Sluggish."

Dan tucked me into his hard body, his palm skimming

along the flat of my stomach. His pinky slid beneath the waistband of my jeans. Apprehension and desire twined together, weakening my once strong resolve. He mouthed my earlobe, and I almost hit the floor.

Through the crack in the door, Brandon paced the kitchen—he appeared like clockwork, then spun and disappeared again. He was at turns bitching and moaning and whining into the cell phone crooked against his ear. "Just tell Dr. Bronner I called." He hung up and leaned against the kitchen counter for a moment, then he disappeared from view.

Dan whispered, "I need to be inside you, but that'll wait." He lapped the tendons on my neck, knowing I liked it, his tongue sliding.

Realization dawned. "Jesus. You're the one who's into this. It's not me wanting to be caught—it's you. It turns you on."

His chest rumbled behind me. "It does." And then he squeezed my dick. I hardened immediately, lengthening to fill his big hand. "And you want it too."

"I..." How the fuck did he get anything done? He was some kind of sex addict.

My cock pulsed in his hand.

He whispered thickly, "Brandon could open the door at any moment. Could come back here and see you with your thick cock in my hand."

"You're crazy."

He had my number though, because his words were working. I started to shake a clear no, but...goddamn it, it *was* exciting. I was stiff as a board, my head light. Here was a man who got off on pursuing me, he had me trapped, and his hand was rubbing my crotch in sure, strong strokes. Heat pooled in my nuts and...maybe caught in the closet with Dan was exactly what I'd been missing lately. I'd quit my job and I was probably going to get arrested. I needed something positive to happen today. I could do this and no one would be the wiser. I mean, we'd already done it once and not gotten caught. What was a second time? Maybe this time around, I could come in three seconds.

I laid my head back on his shoulder, acquiescing. He gently kissed inside my collar, whispering, "That's it," and I couldn't help it, I smiled.

His lips settled hot and wet on my skin, exploring the flesh of my neck and shoulder with his teeth, his tongue. I bit my lip. Dan's hand wriggled inside my pants, and my dick knew what I wanted. It reached to meet his hand. I shifted, my eye still trained on the crack of light and the danger just beyond the door.

Brandon passed by again. He set a glass of soda on the counter. His phone was back to his ear, and he had a loaf of bread in his hand and a jar of peanut butter in the crook of his elbow. He was making a sandwich. He dropped his knife twice. He said into the phone, "Tell him to call me. How hard can it be?"

"*Pretty hard,*" Dan murmured. I thrust full out into his hand.

Oh shit he was perfect—and well practiced in jerking off, I was convinced. I gripped the doorframe and nodded against his shoulder. Heat unfurled along the edge of my spine and far inside my ass. He opened my pants and let my cock out in the dark, hot air. His fist enveloped me. That rough palm slid over my crown and then grazed to my root.

"Just let me..." His other hand cinched my balls tight, and the skin of my dick stretched taut. A tremor worked down my thighs. Panting silently, watching Brandon appear and disappear from view chomping on his peanut butter and drinking soda, I worked my hips into Dan's closed fingers. Dry humping. Cramming into the tight heat of his fist. It burned. It burned so good, the friction uncomfortable, but still fucking good.

"You're going to come hard, so hard, come on." He let go of my balls, and gripped me by the neck, jerking my chin all the way back, tipping me. "Open your mouth, Caesar."

I did. I opened wide, closed my eyes and his mouth met mine. His tongue filled me, fucked me, emptied me of air, of thought. A rip of white light and my hole tingled. His hand was so fast now, I was sure the door was shaking in the frame. I didn't care if anyone could hear me now.

"Shhhh." He kissed me, circling my lips, and one long thick finger pressed in. "Suck on me."

I sucked, and come shot out of my cock like a geyser. I came wet and mute and fearful, shaking in his hands. He licked my neck. "You are something else."

I was something, all right. Crazy. That's what. My eyes flew open and from somewhere a bell rang. Was I blacking out? The ringing cut short. Again a buzzing chirp from somewhere in the apartment. Then a knock. I gripped the door, keeping myself from falling.

He covered my mouth with his clean hand. "Cell phone and someone's here."

There was a thud from the other side of the closet, and Dan jerked. "Shit, he's down. What the fuck?"

Trying to force myself back in to the here and now, I leaned a little harder on the door than necessary. There was entirely too much happening for a post-orgasmic burglar to process. "I can't see him."

The goddamn door swung in a heart-stopping jolt. With Dan's hand in my underwear, my pants around my hips, and

183

my dick slathered in semen, we tumbled with nothing to catch ourselves on except each other. Off balance, we rode the door until it hit something solid on the floor. We tipped sideways, landing in a pile about a foot away from Brandon, who was facedown on the wood floor. He twitched.

Dan scrambled to his feet, wiping his hand on his shirt. I guess that was the least of our worries as someone was still banging on the front door. I stuffed myself back into my jeans, appalled that I'd almost landed dick first onto this poor guy.

"Check his pulse." Dan scoped the hallway. "I wish I had my gun." He shifted into his cop persona—coolly efficient. It was startling.

He disappeared into the kitchen. I heard the water run.

Brandon's heartbeat was erratic, he was sweating, but he was breathing on his own. He was out cold. The smell of peanut butter filled the air. His nose was bleeding on the floor and damn, the guy was running a fever. I ran my hands along his back, checking for injuries. "Brandon. Hey. Hey, buddy. Can you hear me?"

Obviously we missed a critical incident while I was having the most intensely exciting orgasm of my life, again, in the hall cupboard.

Dan came back, his face harsh, and handed me a towel. "Roofie. We need to get an ambulance. I bet whoever did this did it to Shep on Friday night as well. Don't touch anything."

I tried to wipe Bran's nose, poor bastard. His sandwich was stuck to his shirt. I peeled it off.

The front door banged again. "Caesar! Open the door!" Jesus. It was my father. "I know you're in there!"

"Everyone out," Dan yelled, but no one moved. He should have said, Ollie ollie oxen free. He strode down the hall banging on doors. "I called the police, they're on their way."

184

That got everyone moving. Doors flew open. Shep came stumbling from the bathroom, his shoes wet. Mallory and Peter crawled out from under the table.

Shep said, "Where's Poppy? Oh my God, what happened to Bran?"

He hadn't made a sound. "Dan thinks someone slipped him a roofie."

"I meant his face."

I sat there blinking at him. "What are you doing here?"

"I saw the van parked on the curb. I thought you were holding out on me." He was hiding something, damn actor, because he seemed utterly sincere. One thing he couldn't hide was the shift in his complexion. He didn't like blood, I remembered, and he'd faint or puke. He was definitely turning green.

"Shep." Dan nodded at Brandon. "I think this is what was done to you the other night."

Shep nodded. "I think so too. Because...I don't go upstairs with people who aren't memorable."

I decided right there that Shep and Jean Luc were perfectly suited.

Dan went to the front door and my father came stomping down the hall, only to stop at the sight of Brandon, unconscious and bleeding on the floor.

Pop pointed at me with two fingers. "You! You need to get outta here right now."

"Who the hell is he?" Peter pointed back at my father with his long skinny index finger. He and Mallory were rumpled and pale.

Mallory seemed confused. "Is he having an allergic reaction to peanut butter? I've seen that before. Look at his face. Did someone call an ambulance?"

Dan spoke to his aunt. They were side by side, and now the resemblance was striking. "I did. Please, Mallory. You need to leave. Everyone." Somewhere on the street emergency vehicles fought the morning traffic with horn blasts.

"I'm sorry, Daniel. I shouldn't have told Peter where you were. He was...is obsessed. I trust you to do your job."

Dan squatted next to me. "Caesar, you need to go. Now." He retrieved Brandon's cell phone from where it lay on the floor and scrolled through his calls with one hand. He made no effort to hide what he was doing. "Missed call from Dr. Bronner. Three unidentified calls. Four calls from Posh Nosh."

"Hey. Where's Poppy?" Shep asked again.

"That's a good question." Dan's face was hard. "She cut and run."

We all turned and stared at the back door. It was wide open.

"Poppy didn't do this."

"Of course not," my father piped in. He gave Dan a chilling look. "She's like a daughter to me. You watch yourself."

"We'll see."

And then the cops were coming in the front door, and we all fled like rats from a sinking vessel into the alley. My father nabbed my collar and yanked me in the opposite direction. "You don't go with those people."

"I have to move the van." But when we turned the corner, Poppy's pink delivery truck was gone.

# Chapter Twelve:
# Palette of Clowns

My father and I walked back to Rocco's and I told him everything. How it seemed Brandon might be framing Poppy, how Poppy was broke, how my boss had stolen a painting from Mallory, and now it was missing—

"Enough." My father threw his hands in the air. "That man with the swollen face, he works for Poppy—he was her muscle, you know, he's the one who goes and sees people pay her. Nothing illegal, he's the man who checks in. He was strong-armed by someone else."

I nodded. "Yeah."

"You need Tino?"

"No, but thanks anyway."

He sucked his lip. "Joey give you that idea to break in?"

"The door was actually open—"

"Caesar, you're the most honest, loyal person I ever met. You work hard. You look after your grandmother, you take care of Poppy, you make that boss look good—but you're the worst liar in the state of New York. No breaking the law. Hear me?"

I sighed. "Yeah, Pop. I know."

"Joey. He's in law school now. He oughtta know better. You

know he's seeing Poppy?"

"What?"

"See. You need to get out more. Have some fun. You mark my words. They're gonna get married."

"Poppy Romano? No way."

"You'll see." He gave me a bag of cannoli, a hot veal parmesan sandwich, an ice-cold San Pellegrino, and he loaded me into a cab. He paid my fare. He was my pop. I sat digesting the union of Poppy McNamara and Joey Romano, while my father tried to send me off with words of wisdom. "You never ask for help from nobody, you know? But the people who love you want to help you. So you let them. That's what family does. You go find Poppy. She's a good girl. And you tell that Dan he better wise up. You need him to watch your back. Understood?"

Fifteen minutes later the cabbie deposited me in front of the gallery. It should be open, but the doors were locked tight and the studios were dark. Peter was neglecting his duties. Color me surprised.

I walked down the alley. Captain and Joseph sat in their usual spot, the cardboard filthy and stained. It was sunny and it was lunchtime. They were eating gyros wrapped in oily tinfoil. Joseph's nose was buried in another steamy romance novel. A scrawny flea-bitten kitten scratched at its ears between them. "Did you...get a cat?"

"Ayup." Joseph stroked the white fur ball. It had to be crawling with vermin. "She come out of the dumpster." He fed her a tiny sliver of lamb.

"She needs kitten food. That'll make her sick."

"Got some. This be her treat."

Captain reached into the pocket of his buffalo plaid coat, and I stepped warily away. He withdrew a scrap of paper and handed it to me. His hand touched mine. Was it the same one he'd used to blow his nose? I didn't flinch. I took the note carefully between my fingertips. "We wrote down what we remember. You seem like a nice guy."

I unfolded the paper and struggled to read what it said. They'd tried, but penmanship wasn't their strong suit. "Well. Thank you. This is unexpected. And I have something for you, but you can't have it out here."

The men pulled themselves stiffly from the ground, pocketing their gyros. Joseph scooped the pathetic kitten and carried her in the crook of his arm. From the corner of their bedding, a splash of color showed. I couldn't take my eyes off it—splotches of cadmium orange and cobalt blue cerulean contrasted against the bleak shit-brindle-brown of their greasy, filth-stained pallet. If I had to guess, I'd say those were circus colors.

I nudged the cardboard with my foot. "So. The orange guy. He paid you guys to hide a painting?"

The men shifted. They looked at each other, then at me. "Is it stolen?" Captain asked. "We didn't do it. That guy just handed us some money and told us to take it. He said he was comin' back, but he still hadn't come."

Joseph said, "Ain't worth nothin'. Ain't no Modigliani. Or Klee. This is paint-by-number."

"I like Klee too. Can I have that painting? It's someone's mother's. She was partial to it."

Captain bent down and uncovered the canvas. It was smashed from where they'd sat on it, and stained from what I prayed was alcohol and not urine. Captain tried to hand me The Circus of Despair, the subject a sad clown riding an even more tragic carousel horse in a strange muddied tent of woeful onlookers. There appeared to be a juggler and a ringmaster in the background—it was difficult to tell. I could see Peter stealing this, hell, I could picture him humping it while wearing those wing-tipped clown shoes. I shook my white Rocco's takeout bag. "Could you carry it in for me? My hands are full." I was not about to touch that canvas. *Hep C. Typhoid. Rabies!* my mind screamed.

Wordlessly, we climbed the steps to the back door of the gallery, and I unlocked the door and punched the alarm.

Captain stopped at the door. "You bringing us inside? You didn't like dat de other day."

"Well, today's your lucky day. C'mon." They followed me into the kitchen, while their odor followed them.

Captain leaned the missing painting against the wall. Unschooled Acrylic, Dan had said. Mallory was a better bullshit artist than I, for sure, because Salvation Army would have passed on this one. I set my bag on the counter, found the paper plates, a couple forks, and then I carefully unveiled the cannoli. Pop had put a little powdered sugar in a takeout container. I sprinkled that on top and handed the plates to the guys.

"What's dis for?"

"I told you I'd bring you Rocco's. You can't eat my pop's food with your hands. You need a plate. And a fork. You want coffee?"

Captain snatched the plate from my hand as if he feared I'd change my mind. He stared at the dainty pastry. "How many these you got?"

"Four. That's all he could spare. I have napoleon too, if you prefer."

"We'll take the lot. You got soda? I don't like coffee much."

I smiled. "So. Gentlemen. I want to know how this went.

Guy left here with a box and a painting? Or is there someone you're not supposed to tell me about."

Joseph's eyes squinted into slits. He looked to Captain, then back to me. Captain chewed slowly. "We in trouble?"

"No. I just need to know if I'm right. That's all."

Joseph piped in. "Ayup. I didn't see, but the door was propped open wit' a chair or something like. First guy come out and asks us to hide the painting. Gives us fifty bucks and two bottles, and den he say he'll be back later on."

"That was the orange guy?"

"He weren't orange then. And then 'bout half hour later, 'nother guy comes through dat door. Wearing a coat, though, and pushing this huge box."

Two guys. Well my father was right. Brandon wasn't the brains in that outfit—he was most probably the one left to take the fall. Poor bastard. I let the guys take the cannoli outside with their forks, Peter's plates, a couple cans of soda, and the bag of goodies. Captain stuck his hand out. "Thanks...what's your name?"

"Caesar." I shook it. I had Purell.

"Well, you de only decent person dat works in dis place. You're okay. So look it. The guy come back the next morning, and he was orange. He told us to hold on to the painting. We was supposed to leave that envelope with the ear thing...but we forgot so Joseph stuck it on yer truck."

"So it's not really mine, right?"

"I dunno about dat."

"You know," Joseph drawled, "you oughta git yerself a different truck. That one ain't very manly."

I let the men and their kitten outside the back door, handing them a couple creamers for the cat, then I stuck my resignation on the refrigerator with Peter's Andy Warhol magnet and went to Poppy's.

# Chapter Thirteen:
# Frank and Beans

I came around the corner to Posh Nosh. It was well after two and the streets of Manhattan bustled with tourists. The after-lunch crowd had hit the Village. Poppy's place would be doing a fair trade in dessert and coffee.

I was halfway down the street when Rachel stepped from the glass door to Posh Nosh. She was in baggy jeans and a T-shirt, her hair hidden under a ball cap—and from this distance, despite those amazing gravity-defying knockers, she looked more like a striking, effeminate young man than I'd ever noticed. Like a luscious tranny in the broad light of day. She opened the back of a Jeep Cherokee and slid a cardboard box filled with wine into her arms. She was hauling the leftovers from Shep's party out of her brother's car. She lugged the box through the door, disappearing from view.

Dan would meet me any minute now. He'd called to tell me Brandon was stable, somewhat lucid, but scared into silence. My father was right. Someone had their thumb on the bartender/model, and it wasn't my best friend.

I entered the side alley, passing the Posh Nosh van where it was tucked in the narrow lot. On the stoop, where the kitchen door entered the back of her place, Poppy sat on a stack of milk crates, looking wan and smoking a cigarette. Her hair was drawn back, her mouth pinched in anger.

"I thought you quit."

"This? It's an invisible cigarette. I'm not inhaling anyway, just holding it. What's with you, Ce? You never answer the phone."

I shrugged. "I'm tired of people calling me. I thought I'd come by in the flesh. I hear you're seeing my cousin."

"Are you mad? I was afraid you'd be mad."

"Of course not. Do you love him? Or at least, can you stand him?"

She smiled. "I can. He's a lot like you...but different."

"That's the truth. So. Why were you at Brandon's?"

"I went to bitch Brandon out and get my money, right? 'Cause it's apparent to me he's stealing. He was helping with the books—I mean he's getting sort of old to be hauling stuff around, and his face is nearly always swollen, so I asked him to give me a hand around the office. So this morning, I get to Park Slope, and Shep walks in first. I'm so sick of him, you know?" She flicked her ash over the railing, then stared at the butt of her cigarette with longing. She wanted it, but she wouldn't let herself bend. She was in her workday clothes—chef's coat and a pair of black leggings. She had ballet flats on her feet. Her headband was in place. Silver today.

"Tell me about it. Who did he sleep with that mattered to you? Jean?"

"Please. You have to ask?"

"But he did."

She nodded. "Neither one of them gay, right? I brought Jean to Connecticut as my date three frickin' months ago—he only went to schmooze Chad and my folks. So he and Shep excused themselves from the table, like crepe suzette and a mimosa, and then the two of them are in the men's room jacking each other off. Three months later, they're still at it. Three frickin' months. That's why Shep came Friday night—not to see you. I think he's terrified of getting outted, yeah, because of all that money, but he's smitten. Really. He's in love. You should have seen Chad last night when Jean Luc grabbed Shep's ass at the door. I thought Chad was going to have a seizure."

"What the hell was Shep doing at Brandon's apartment this morning?"

"He told me 'bout an hour ago that he thinks Brandon is blackmailing him. He remembered something from the other night—but he was so drunk, he wasn't sure. Shep was there to talk to Bran. My God, Ce, when did he get this bad? He's spinning out of control. His mother's going to kill him."

"No. We were both wrong, he wasn't out of control." I told her about the roofie, the video, and about Brandon's collapse.

"I didn't know." Poppy swallowed and contemplated her cigarette again. "It's like every place I go, my entire life, there's Shep. Since kindergarten. And now I'm reduced to working for him. You're the best thing I ever got from him, Ce."

"Yeah. It goes both ways. Except the oral. He does that exceptionally well."

She smiled. "I just want my money. I called Joey last night and he said someone's ripping me off. Here. At my place. I worked so hard. I was ready to expand, and then...it's like I trusted the wrong people. My own staff. Joey said there's a dummy account under my name—and I know it's Bran. PayPal. I hate PayPal."

"It's insane. It's like someone wants to be caught."

Kitchen noises carried from the screen door. The crew was cleaning the lunch mess. Poppy leaned her slender back against the brick wall. "I'm so tired. I thought I could do all this on my own, and I'm tired."

I slid a milk crate over and sat beside her. "Yeah. You need me."

Poppy started to cry. Big fat tears spilled from her lashes, her blue eyes swimming. Her nose didn't run and neither did her mascara. "I do. I need you. I can't do this by myself and...if Joey can figure out where my money went...I want to get back to normal and I want to know...if you'll help me. I'm good at the cooking, but the rest of it is a nightmare."

"I quit today, so I'm looking for a new venture. I thought a bankrupt catering company in Manhattan during the economic downturn would be just the ticket."

She smiled bravely. "Would you? Please?"

"Of course. All you have to do is ask and I will." We digested my newfound career opportunity. Managing a catering company? This I could do. Do well. And enjoy. I was a Romano, after all.

She said, "I'll pay you half."

"Of nothing? Well, it's twice as much as I'm making now."

She reached and squeezed my hand. "Brace yourself, because I swear to God, I think I'm pregnant."

Before I could react to that bombshell, a stack of plates fell behind us, and we both strained to see through the screen. "Fuck! Fuck!" Rachel screamed from the kitchen.

We stumbled over each other trying to get inside. I let my eyes adjust to the fluorescent lighting. Rachel stood at the far sink twisting a towel around her hand. "Sorry. Oh my God. Poppy. What the hell? Are you shitting me? I never thought—I just never suspected that you'd get yourself knocked up."

The kitchen door burst wide and Shep, looking dapper and

tan and more confused than I'd seen him since we took Calculus as freshmen, charged in with his mouth hanging open. His beautiful head swiveled, taking us all in. "You." He pointed at Rachel.

Rachel blanched and carefully moved back with a crunch. Broken crockery covered the floor between her and Shep. For the first time in my memory, she wasn't wearing heels.

Shep stared at the towel in Rachel's hand. "It was you. I remember now. We were in the office and you..." He swallowed sickly.

Poppy's eyes were round as saucers. She said, "Oh my God. It's you."

Everything snapped into place while Rachel, her hair still stuck under the cap, her face devoid of makeup, a tiny wisp of hair above her lip—suddenly became a boy. Right there. In front of my nose. Tits and all. I glanced at the crotch of Rachel's jeans. I mean, I couldn't possibly help myself from taking a peek. If she had a package, it wasn't noteworthy. Clearly *she* wasn't Italian. "Rachel?"

She gave me a hard-eyed stare as the towel on her hand pinkened with blood. "Ce?" she said sweetly, eyes wide. "So you're going to be the new boss. Like I work here for two years doing every single thing, making sure Poppy looks good and paying the bills and cleaning the floors and keeping all these boys in line, doing the schedule, and you're going to be my new boss?"

"Where's Justin Timberlake?"

"Wouldn't you like to know?" Catty bitch.

Poppy threw her cigarette butt in the sink. "Fuck the head. Where's my goddamn money?"

No wonder Shep had no clue what happened. Boy or girl, I'd asked. I was having a hard time processing with Shep gasping for air and getting ill beside me. He wasn't on the verge of violence. No, the blood on Rachel's hand was having its usual effect on him. He waved on his feet.

"Shep. Put your head between your knees before you fall down."

Rachel sneered at him. "You are such a pussy."

He was, but the poor bastard was reeling. Words flew out of my mouth before I could stop them. "You oughtta know."

Rachel's eyes got mean, she stood tall, and I gotta tell you, she was bigger and stronger than both Poppy and I because she'd been hauling the warming oven, with Justin's head in it, up and down the stairs. She carried crates of glasses and plates in four-inch heels. She slung trays and loaded trucks. She was ripped. Those enormous breasts, the makeup, the trash jewelry, the over-sexualized walk, all that cherry-flavored lip goo—I mean there was no way I'd have thought she was preoperative if Shep hadn't had sex with her. She was just...such a girl.

"How the hell did you think you were going to get away with this?"

She shrugged and smiled.

"Oh my God. You were just going to leave Brandon holding the bag. You set him up."

Rachel tied the towel into a knot on her cut with one hand and her teeth. "Bran was trying to pay for all the surgery, and then he got religion or something. Said he was worried about Poppy and was going to tell her the truth. Well, I'm not going to jail."

"He let you down, so you double-crossed him? That's pathetic."

"You whore. You stole my fucking money." Poppy snatched a plate and threw it at Rachel's head. She grabbed another and flung it like a Frisbee at Rachel's neck. Fast, Rachel dodged them both. Crockery smashed under her Converse as she came at Poppy. Poppy. Five foot even and a hundred pounds soaking wet. Shep was too busy gagging into the sink and trying to keep upright to help. Poppy reached for a frying pan, but I grabbed Rachel by her ponytail as she passed and swung her around, smashing her head into the dishwasher. Her bloody hand snaked up to latch onto my wrist, her fist swung to my gut, her foot stomped on my instep, and I kneed that bitch in the nuts with all my strength. I popped her balls—no surgery required.

She doubled over, puking onto the floor.

Poppy cracked her on the head with her pan and like that, Rachel was out.

"Oh my God. Did I kill her?" Poppy was panting and flushed. "Oh my God." She snorted and covered her mouth with her hand. She snorted again and wiped silver hair from her brow. "That was amazing. Jesus, you took her down."

I checked Rachel's pulse. I was proficient at that activity now. "You should call the cops."

Shep slid to the floor. "Christ, Ce. That was incredible. I think I'm going to be sick." He leaned into the wall, eyes closed. "I'm pretty sure she tried to kill Brandon."

"Me too."

The kitchen door swung and Dan came into the room with a plate of quiche in one hand and a phone pressed to his ear. He glanced down at Rachel and then Shep. "What the hell is going on back here? Romano, every time I turn around you're one step ahead of me and neck deep in something."

"Five thousand dollars for breast augmentation," was all I could think to say. "Shep thought he'd followed a girl upstairs, but he was so drugged, he couldn't remember."

Shep said weakly, "The video was the real thing."

"That's just gross...I don't mean to sound like a prude, but..." Poppy gazed between us. "What? You were thinking the same thing."

Dan turned to Shep. "I bagged the condom. You can press charges—or Brandon will. No one needs to find out anything else."

I said to Dan, "I bet she owed that Dr. Bronner a load of money, she and Brandon."

He nodded. "She had us all snowed. I came here to talk to her. She and Jean Luc were the only ones unaccounted for."

"Brandon. Man. Talk about being led around by your dick." That idiot.

Poppy tilted her head, staring at Rachel where she lay sprawled on the floor. "You know. I'm tempted to peek in her pants to see what she has under there."

Dan and I both yelled, "No! *No!*"

# Chapter Fourteen:
# Neat With a Bow

We met back at the gallery at five. It seemed like common ground for Jean Luc, Mallory and Peter. Poppy brought her famous raspberry cake with the chocolate ganache and I brewed a pot of Fog Lifter, my last one at the Stuhlmann gallery. Joey arrived with a fistful of white roses and his best shirt. He was freshly shaved, and he'd made free with his discount Bulgari *Aqua Pour Homme*. He kissed Poppy right in front of me and then he drew me aside.

"I love that girl."

Before he could say another word, I cut him off. "I do too. I could kill you right here with my bare hands. You lying to me, Joey, because I swear to God..." I poked his chest hard with my index finger. "You better do right by her. *Capisce?*"

"*Capisce.* Hey, that was good. Very old school, you know? Sort of butch. You're like her brother, and I understand. But, uh, where's Uncle Rocco's lock pick? Your father's pissed like nobody's business."

"Ain't that the truth?"

Dan sauntered into the kitchen, his boots scuffing the floor. He had Justin Timberlake's head in a box. Poor bastard's ear and nipple were missing. His Swatch eyes were cracked.

Peter winced at the ruined bust, twisting a napkin in his manicured hands. "You can't quit, Caesar. I need you."

Dan's eyes met mine from where he stood by the door. He winked encouragingly, his smile letting that dimple make an appearance, and I winked back. There was just something about him that I hadn't ever known in my past relationships. Honesty maybe? Openness? Pride? He was clear that we were involved—or that he wanted us to be involved. He was pursuing me openly—in front of my family, even. He was loud and proud and in on all my secrets. He seemed to appreciate me more in spite of them. Something fluttered around inside my chest. Something unprecedented. I turned to Peter. "Quit? I can and I did. It's been a good few years, but I'm ready to move on."

"It's so sudden. What am I supposed to do?"

"I guess you'll have to run the gallery yourself until you can find an assistant," Poppy chimed in. "I mean, it can't be that hard if you pay so little. I'm sure some clown will come and take over."

Peter's mouth turned down. He said crossly, "That's not funny."

Mallory entered dressed in her expected black pencil skirt and tailored jacket. She immediately noticed the painting where it rested forlornly against the neat wall. Her manicured fingers clutched the top button on her silk blouse. "Oh thank God."

Dan nodded to his aunt, handing her a cup of coffee. "It was here all along, in the alley. Rachel swiped it from Peter's storage facility, and Brandon gave it to the bums for safekeeping. I don't think Brandon ever told her where it was. He was hoping for leverage and his plan backfired."

Mallory glared at Peter. "You are so fortunate. This painting is worth millions to the Albright."

We all stared at the urine-stained canvas. Dan said, "I hope that pee comes out."

"We have people for that." Mallory sniffed. "I can't thank you enough, Daniel."

Shep arrived on those words, Jean Luc close by his side. The pair looked suspiciously relaxed—as if they'd had sex in the cab on the way over. Shep seemed a bit too cool which was a dead giveaway to me. If ever there was a man for Shep, I'd say it was Jean Luc. "Hey, Caesar found the painting. He should get the reward."

"Reward?" There was a reward?

"It's five thousand dollars." Mallory reached into her Coach bag and handed me a flyer. "I just had these printed. It was Sheppard's idea. We were desperate."

Five thousand dollars? Because of Shep—of all people. Poppy grinned at me and muttered a tiny "Yes!" along with an unrepentant fist pump.

Peter swallowed audibly. "So Rachel stole the painting from upstairs?"

Shep handed Jean a cup of coffee, then he grabbed one for himself. "I remember that she came down the stairs with the painting. I was lying on the floor in Peter's office. I remember her polka-dot skirt and that's it. Oh. She dragged me down the hall by my feet. That chick is strong."

Dan said, "Rachel gave the painting to Brandon and he left, propping the chair in the door for her. He thought she was here having sex with Peter, but she was busy stealing Justin Timberlake. She rolled the bust right out the back door in that oven and loaded him into her car. Pretending to be a victim was pretty smart."

"Pretending to be a girl was even smarter," Poppy added.

"She fooled me. Shit she fooled everyone." I never

questioned Rachel, even when I knew the truth about her...condition. Dr. Bronner had certainly earned his five thousand dollars.

Dan came to stand beside me. His shirt sleeve brushed my arm, and I tried to squelch the tiny thrill his touch gave me. "There is no brother. That was her cover. She is Roger, not Rachel."

"And she tried to kill Bran," Poppy said. She and Joey stood by the sink. His arms were around her waist, and she was nestled into his body. I was having a hard time adjusting, but I'd survive. Poppy went on, "She wanted it to look like he was the one blackmailing everyone. She was going to get off scot-free."

Dan nodded. "She was going to disappear and take the money."

"God what a freaking bitch," Joey said. "Who's this chick again? I might know someone who could pay her a visit—"

"That's not necessary." I smiled nervously at my cousin, giving him the well-known shut-the-fuck-up look. "We're letting the law handle this."

He shrugged. "I guess that's good too."

Peter said, "I knew there was something weird about that girl."

I had to know. I'm sure everyone was wondering the same thing, so I came right out and asked. "Did you...uhm...see her...parts?"

The room grew silent as we waited with bated breath to hear Peter's response. He stared at the wall clock and flushed to his roots. His silver hair gleamed in contrast. He muttered, "No. I had a...medical problem...which I'd forgotten my, er, medication for, so we called it an evening right after you left."

Dan coughed into the silence. "Cake anyone?"

We pounced on the cake and coffee, talking about anything except Peter's erectile dysfunction.

Mallory came near. "Caesar, I want to let you know that the assistant position is open at the Albright, and I'd be quite happy if you took the job. You'd be an excellent fit for the Albright."

"Thank you, Mallory. I appreciate that. However, I'm going to try a new venture."

"Me too, Caesar." Jean lifted his cup and announced, "Here's to Chad Schumacher."

I spit my coffee out. Dan calmly handed me a napkin. "*Grazie.*"

Jean went on, "I've been commissioned to create a bust of Mr. Potter."

Shep nodded happily, his platinum hair undulating around his exquisitely handsome face. "I'll be sitting for that."

No kidding.

Jean used the flat of his palm to toy with his nipple ring, which was completely unnecessary. "He'll be doing more than sitting." He leered. "If you know what I mean."

"I believe we do." What a pair.

Poppy stuck her knife deeply into the cake. "So what's this mean? You two are together now? In public?" She pointed between them with the raspberry-covered knife. "What about *Mr. Potter?* You going to do it, Shep? Gonna let Auntie Cricket and Uncle Beau know that you like to play with boys?"

Shep turned a bright vermillion red. "We've been together since that afternoon at the country club. Jean and I." And fuck me if Jean didn't actually reach out to squeeze Shep's hand. I looked to Dan, whose warm eyes watched me carefully. I smiled crookedly at him. Shep blathered on, "I'm sorry, Caesar. I...was upset about Rachel because I'd come to the gallery to see Jean Friday night, it's true. I didn't know what happened—and I didn't want to ruin this good thing by doing something so stupid. I thought I'd let him down."

Poppy glared at him. "Shep, goddammit, you're going to have to let Schumacher know the truth."

"I told Estelle she's handling it or she's fired. That's her job. They've splashed my face on every bus and billboard in New York, so I don't think they'll let me go. I think..." he grinned sheepishly, "...I think I may have a book deal. It's a lot of money."

"That's my boy!" Jean laughed heartily.

# Epilogue

He who is brave is free.

~*Seneca*

Dan and I crossed the Verrazano Narrows Bridge at seventy miles per hour. Zipped once again in his leather jacket, the cool night embraced me. I let my arms fall on his hips, my hands settle on his hard thighs. My fears, tonight, I put to rest.

The sky was blanketed in yellow haze, but beyond that, the city lights twinkled like the Milky Way. Who needed the real thing when we had this multicolored galaxy spread before us blazing with possibility? It was breathtaking, and outside, at this speed, I felt ready to take on something new.

We only stopped to pay the toll, which was surprisingly cheap for a hometown boy on two wheels, and then we were cruising into Staten Island, following the highway to that now-familiar Richmond Road exit.

We were going to have sex at his house. I mean, where else would we go?

By the time we arrived at the Green residence, my thighs were shaking. I climbed off the Harley gingerly, careful not to fall on the driveway like a fool.

"So. You like the bike?"

LB Gregg

I nodded. "I do, actually. It's more fun than I expected. Maybe I could drive it sometime."

His mouth twitched. "We'll see. Maybe. If you're good."

"I'm always good, Dan Green Albright. You're the lawbreaker."

"So figure it out, Romano. That's a yes."

We went into the house, throwing our jackets on the painted banister. My hands were cold and I flexed them, knuckles cracking in the still house.

"Do you want a beer?"

I shook my head, and with a deep breath and a shove, I knocked that new man in my life onto the couch. He smiled, surprised when I straddled his lap, my thighs spread over his. I tried for sexy. "Nope. What I want is to...to... I want..." But Christ, I couldn't dirty talk to save my life. I could, however, stutter with the best of them. I slumped, my forehead resting against his. "Shit."

Dan smiled, smug as hell. "What do you want? You want to fuck me?"

"Yes. That. Then I want to take a shower and maybe, if you'd like, I'll spend the night and we can...do that again in the morning. I brought a toothbrush. And tomorrow you can make waffles."

"Sure thing. Whatever you want, Caesar. You know that I'm sworn to serve."

I let my fingers trail through his black hair. "So. I just want to say, before we do this thing, that I think—"

All humor gone, he gripped me by the back of the neck, his eyes narrowing fiercely. "Are you still looking for an excuse not to let this thing happen between us?"

"I'm sitting on your lap, in your house, and I have a hard-

208

on. What makes you think I'm not letting this thing happen?"

He ground his pelvis into me. "I like you sitting on my lap."

"Yeah. I got that."

His voice turned rough with honesty. "I have no lies, no secrets, what do you want to know? The scars? Fire. On the job. I got a settlement. I left the force. You know any out cops? No. I didn't enjoy being the only one, so I took my cash, and this house, and I'm free."

"Free? Define free."

Dan's eyes darkened, his hand lingered on my neck and he drew me in. I plastered my chest against his, gripping his shoulders in my cold hands. His words rumbled against me. "I'm free to start something with this hot piece of ass I tasted the other night."

"Yeah. Hot, huh? You like my hot piece of ass, Albright?" My face must have flamed purple. Dan's eyes widened in surprise, but he looked overjoyed. This was fun, actually. "What?"

"Well, look at you. Mr. Dirty Talk."

"I can be butch."

"Mmm-hmm. If you say so."

His dick was pressed into the crutch of my legs and I wormed my hand into his jeans. I whispered, "Let's take these off you," exactly as he had to me. His smile tickled against my lips. I licked the seam of his mouth, and he let me in with a laugh.

"You hoping to lead me around by my dick tonight?"

"Something like that." I kissed him before he could comment, because surely he had something more to add. With one hand I fondled that heavy, big-headed treat swelling inside his jeans, and with the other I fisted his thick hair. I licked and tasted Dan—mint, coffee, chocolate, the night air, the heat of his mouth, the sweet flavor of need. I sucked his tongue, nipped his lower lip and worried his smooth skin. His lips were firm, but giving, and in that moment, he was all those things I most wanted in a lover. The scratch of whiskers against mine, the tight, muscular flesh under my hands, the hairy pits and broad chest, the sharp jaw, the big hand gripping my ass—currently stealing its way into my underwear—that smell of leather and soap, the strength, the physicality. The humor. That irritating smile and the know-it-all wink.

Shit. I had it bad.

He pushed me away, eyes twinkling. "We'll see, Romano. I may have some other plans tonight. I can't seem to get enough of this. It's all I thought about. All day. All yesterday." His fingers grazed my cleft, reaching deep. His fingertips wanted inside me, and that was exciting and terrifying and electrifying. I'd have to think about it. He murmured against my lips, "Little virgin ass. I feel like it's mine. Like two days, and damn, you belong to me. I can't get enough of you." He leaned in and kissed me again, this time sliding forward. And then he literally tossed me from his lap. "But, hey, I wouldn't want to stop you from your goal, Romano. Far be it from me to stand in your way." He offered me that wink.

I sank between his legs, letting him relax into the cushions, and dragged his pants down just enough to let his erection out. It was wide and purple-capped and veined and wet on the top. I gripped that monster in one hand and set his velvety skin against my lips. I was exactly where I wanted to be right now, in this position on my knees, letting him have my mouth. Never, ever had I felt so...partnered. Lead him around by his dick? No. I wanted to lead him by the hand.

I caught his brown-eyed gaze, his expression made my own pants a bit too tight in the crotch, and I drew him into my mouth, slow and steady, tasting his salt. I swallowed and tightened, and he moaned, raw. "That's it, Caesar, suck my dick. Use your tongue."

I did. His eyes drifted closed, his soot-black lashes long against his cheek, his mouth tense, his jaw set grimly in that concentrated *please God don't let him stop sucking my dick* line men get when they want to come more than anything else in the entire world. He thrust sharp and rude into my face. His hands dug into my hair, and for a heartbeat he lost all control. I let him choke me with his cock. Then his hands flopped onto his thighs and he sighed. "Sorry. I don't mean to be rough. Jesus. You're just so perfect. Deeper, Ce. Go deep, baby."

Since he asked so politely, I took it all. I'd spent the last few encounters with Dan doing my own mumbling and begging, so here was Dan's comeuppance. He was purring against me. I squeezed around him, one hand slipped down to hold his sac and I set a pace pushing to win. His thighs grew tense and then with a heaving heavy lift of his pelvis—he came hard in a quick squirt of ocean-flavored milk right down the back of my tongue. He spurted his load, his legs trembled, and I quietly swallowed, letting him finish until he slumped back into the couch with a goofy smile on his face.

I laid my head on his thigh, and his hand felt my hair, combing through, stroking me in that sure way of his. He got his breath back, and he hauled me to my feet. He stuffed his soft prick into his pants, and then he winked and kissed me. "You can lead me by the dick any time you want, Romano. Just know that your turn is coming."

"Promises, promises." Naturally, my stomach chose that moment to growl. I hadn't eaten since Poppy's cake. "But first, I think you should feed me."

"I thought I just did."

"You're such an ass, Albright."

He took my hand, pulling me toward the kitchen. "Yeah, but if you want it, it's all yours, Romano."

# About the Author

LB Gregg began writing in the spring of 2008 at the encouragement of author pal, Josh Lanyon. She never once looked back (although occasionally she looked down and tripped over her own feet). 2009 saw the publication of her best selling Men of Smithfield series.

LB lives in the Connecticut hills with two lazy dogs, three above-average children, and a smoking hot husband who, thank the good Lord, loves to cook.

You can find LB at her blog, Noseinabook: http://lisabea.blogspot.com or visit her website www.lbgregg.com.

*A vacation fling. No complications. No connections.*
*And no regrets.*

# No Souvenirs
## © *2010 K.A. Mitchell*

Trauma surgeon Jae Sun Kim has just lost the job he wanted more than anything else in his life. Looking for a way to hit the reset button, he takes a scuba vacation. He didn't plan on seasickness, or a dive master who is sex-on-the-beach personified.

Shane McCormack's tendency to drift away from complicated situations has landed him a job as a dive master in Belize, which isn't as glamorous as it sounds. But with the big three-oh looming, asking his parents to bail him out again isn't an option. The job isn't without its perks, though, and as soon as he figures a way to keep that hot but arrogant ass of a doctor from tossing his cookies over the side of the boat, he plans to flirt the control freak out of his brittle shell.

The close quarters on the ship generate more heat than either expects, but a vacation fling is all that's in the plans. An unexpected adventure leaves them changed in ways that make it impossible to go back to their old lives. The risks they'll both have to take could leave them with nothing but more scars, or the best souvenir of all.

*Warning: This title contains m/m snark and sex. If you experience side effects from reading about either of these activities, please consult a physician before reading.*

*Available now in ebook and print from Samhain Publishing.*

LaVergne, TN USA
14 January 2011

212444LV00009B/9/P